Dear Reader,

We're thrilled that some of your favorite families are making an encore appearance! With this special Famous Families fifty-book collection, we are proud to offer you the chance to relive the drama, the glamour, the suspense and the romance of four of Harlequin's most beloved families— the Fortunes, the Bravos, the McCabes and the Cavanaughs.

You'll begin your journey at the Double Crown ranch in Red Rock, Texas, home of the legendary Fortunes and the setting of the twelve-book miniseries Fortunes of Texas: Reunion. Members of the family are preparing to honor their patriarch, Ryan Fortune, but a bloodred moon offers a portent of trouble ahead. As the clan deals with a mysterious body, an abduction, a health crisis and numerous family secrets, each member also manages to find love and a happily-ever-after you'll want to share.

We hope you enjoy your time in Red Rock. Be prepared for our next stop, the Rising Sun Ranch in Medicine Creek, Wyoming, where *USA TODAY* bestselling author Christine Rimmer kicks off the story of the Bravo family. Watch for *The Nine-Month Marriage*, the first of the Bravo series, beginning in March!

Happy reading,

The Editors

SHERI WHITEFEATHER

is a bestselling author who has won numerous awards, including readers' and reviewer's choice honors. She writes a variety of romance novels for Harlequin Books. She has become known for incorporating Native American elements into her stories. She has two grown children, who are tribally enrolled members of the Muscogee Creek Nation.

Sheri is of Italian-American descent. Her great-grandparents immigrated to the United States from Italy through Ellis Island, originating from Castel di Sangro and Sicily. She lives in California and enjoys ethnic dining, shopping in vintage stores and going to art galleries and museums.

Sheri loves to hear from her readers. Visit her website at www.SheriWhiteFeather.com.

FAMOUS FAMILIES

the FORTUNES

SHERI WHITEFEATHER

Once a Rebel

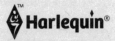

Harlequin®

TORONTO NEW YORK LONDON
AMSTERDAM PARIS SYDNEY HAMBURG
STOCKHOLM ATHENS TOKYO MILAN MADRID
PRAGUE WARSAW BUDAPEST AUCKLAND

Special thanks and acknowledgment are given to
Sheri WhiteFeather for her contribution to the
Fortunes of Texas: Reunion series.

To Patience Smith (our amazing editor) and the other authors on this
series—seeing you in Dallas was a blast.
To those who weren't able to be there, we missed you.

Recycling programs
for this product may
not exist in your area.

ISBN-13: 978-0-373-36488-6

ONCE A REBEL

FAMOUS FAMILIES

The Fortunes

Cowboy at Midnight by Ann Major
A Baby Changes Everything by Marie Ferrarella
In the Arms of the Law by Peggy Moreland
Lone Star Rancher by Laurie Paige
The Good Doctor by Karen Rose Smith
The Debutante by Elizabeth Bevarly
Keeping Her Safe by Myrna Mackenzie
The Law of Attraction by Kristi Gold
Once a Rebel by Sheri WhiteFeather
Military Man by Marie Ferrarella
Fortune's Legacy by Maureen Child
The Reckoning by Christie Ridgway

The Bravos by Christine Rimmer

The Nine-Month Marriage
Marriage by Necessity
Practically Married
Married by Accident
The Millionaire She Married
The M.D. She Had to Marry
The Marriage Agreement
The Bravo Billionaire
The Marriage Conspiracy
His Executive Sweetheart
Mercury Rising
Scrooge and the Single Girl

The McCabes by Cathy Gillen Thacker

Dr. Cowboy
Wildcat Cowboy
A Cowboy's Woman
A Cowboy Kind of Daddy
A Night Worth Remembering
The Seven-Year Proposal
The Dad Next Door
The Last Virgin in Texas
Texas Vows: A McCabe Family Saga
The Ultimate Texas Bachelor
Santa's Texas Lullaby
A Texas Wedding Vow
Blame It on Texas
A Laramie, Texas Christmas
From Texas, With Love

The Cavanaughs by Marie Ferrarella

Racing Against Time
Crime and Passion
Internal Affair
Dangerous Games
The Strong Silent Type
Cavanaugh's Woman
In Broad Daylight
Alone in the Dark
Dangerous Disguise
The Woman Who Wasn't There
Cavanaugh Watch
Cavanaugh Heat

Chapter 1

Susan Fortune approached the barn, the weathered wood calling to her like an old friend, stirring scattered memories, making them swirl in her mind.

In the past seventeen years she hadn't been home much. She'd returned now and then, but always in a rush, a day or two at Thanksgiving, Christmas or Easter. But being back in Red Rock, Texas, back on the Double Crown Ranch, felt different this time.

Because this wasn't a harried holiday weekend, a fast-paced trip she'd crammed into her busy schedule. This was the real thing. A homecoming that turned her heart inside out.

Her cousin Ryan, the Fortune family patriarch, was dying.

Susan moved closer to the barn, the slightly chilled, early February air stinging her skin. She'd spent the most important time of her life, her senior year in high school, on the Double Crown. Ryan had taken her in after her alcohol-enraged father had kicked her out. He'd offered her a place to stay, a place to feel loved, a home away from home, from the turbulence that had nearly destroyed her.

And now here she was, wishing she could save Ryan, but knowing she couldn't.

Reflective, she looked around, watching the ranch hands do their jobs. And then a tall, tanned man in rugged denims, with a straw cowboy hat dipped low on his forehead, exited the barn. He strode toward a white dually, and suddenly she couldn't breathe, every ounce of oxygen in her lungs refusing to cooperate.

Was that Ethan Eldridge?

Yes, she told herself. It had to be. He'd grown bigger, broader, more masculine, but she recognized him just the same. Even the way he wore his clothes bred familiarity. A hand-tooled belt that he'd probably made himself was threaded through his jeans, and the hem of each pant leg frayed around a pair of weather-beaten boots. When he adjusted his hat in a memorable manner, her girl-hood dreams went up in a cloud of pheromone-scented smoke.

She hadn't seen him since they were teenagers, since she'd pined for him like the emotionally torn, desperate-for-affection female she'd been.

Should she call his name? Get his attention before he climbed into his truck and drove away?

Or would that make her look foolish? Susan Fortune, the reformed bad girl, flaunting herself in front of Ethan Eldridge all over again.

Unsure of what to do, she simply stood where she was, the wind whipping her hair across her cheek. But before she could come to a decision, Ethan reacted to her presence. Like a solitary animal, a cougar sensing an intruder, he slowed his pace and turned around.

Leaving Susan exposed to his gaze.

Chiding herself, she smoothed her hair, batting it away from her face. She wasn't reverting to pro-miscuity. If anything, she was able to diagnose her teenage self, the rebellious girl who'd paraded other boys in front of Ethan. Susan understood the wild child that had festered inside her. She'd graduated from Stanford and earned a Ph.D. in psychology.

She decided to greet him with a friendly yet noncommittal hello, so she started off in his direction, cutting across the dirt path that separated them. But as she analyzed his catlike posture, she realized that he hadn't identified her.

He had no idea who she was.

Beneath the brim of his hat, his eyebrows furrowed. A frown of curiosity, she thought. A country boy wondering why a citified blonde, dressed in designer jeans and a form-fitting blazer, was determined to talk to him.

Finally when they were face-to-face, with sights, sounds and smells of the ranch spinning around them, recognition dawned in his eyes.

Those stunning blue eyes.

"Susan?" He beat her to the punch, saying her name first.

"Ethan." She extended her hand, preparing to touch him. "It's good to see you."

"You, too." He accepted her hand, enveloping it with callused fingers.

They gazed at each other, silence sizzling between them. She could feel the soundless energy zapping the air, conjuring invisible fireflies.

So much for her Ph.D.

Suddenly she was a smitten seventeen-year-old, reliving the day they'd met. He had been a ranch hand's hardworking, properly reared son, and she had been as untamed as the Texas terrain, a lost girl aching for attention. So much so, she'd parked her butt on a fence rail, as close to him as possible. Then she'd unbuttoned the top of her blouse, complaining about the heat, trying to get him to look at her.

He did, but only for a second. Just long enough to stop working and offer her a bottle of water. His water. A plastic container he'd yet to open, to drink from.

An elusive boy. A gallant gesture.

In her young, needy soul, Susan had fallen like a ton of shattered bricks, wanting Ethan even more. But she'd never gotten him. Nothing. Not even a kiss.

"I'm sorry about what's happening to Ryan," he said, bringing her back to the present. "You know how much I care about him."

She nodded. Ethan had practically grown up on the Double Crown. He knew Ryan well. "He's such a good man. Everyone loves him."

"I'm sure he's glad to have you home."

Home. The word never failed to strike her heart. She'd lived with her parents in Katy, Texas, a suburb of Houston, until Ryan took her in. Sixteen years in Katy and one year in Red Rock. Yet Red Rock would always seem like home, even though she'd moved away from Texas altogether.

Ethan shifted his stance, drawing her attention to his tall, muscular form. He'd been lean and wiry as a teenager, a boy who'd spent all of his free time with the animals on the ranch.

"Ryan told me you became a large-animal vet," she said.

"And he told me you became a child psychologist." A smile ghosted across his lips. "I guess we both grew up, didn't we?"

"Yes, we did." As a girl, she used to dream about that uneven smile. Slow and sexy, she thought. One corner of his mouth tilting in a lazy sort of way.

Caught up in the moment, she stole a glance at his left hand. The last she'd heard, he was single, but that was a few years ago. She hadn't made a habit of grilling Ryan about him.

When she noticed the absence of a ring, she sighed. Ethan was thirty-five, the same age as she was, and she'd never married, either. But her work was her priority, the heartbeat of her existence.

Did Ethan feel that way, too? Or was she jumping to conclusions? Just because he didn't wear a ring didn't mean he wasn't involved in a committed relationship. Or that he wasn't looking for a partner, someone to share the ups and downs in his life.

"Did you just get here today?" he asked.

"Yes." She told herself to quit psychoanalyzing him, to leave her textbook curiosity at the curb. "I arrived this morning." She flipped her wrist and checked her watch. "A few hours ago. Ryan is taking a nap, so I decided to go for a walk."

"How's Lily holding up?"

"She's doing the best she can. When I left the house, she was fussing in the kitchen, giving herself something to do." Lily was Ryan's third wife, a woman he'd loved since his youth but hadn't married until many years later.

The wind rustled Ethan's shirt. "How long are you going to stay?"

"I'm not sure. But I'm hoping to help everyone get through this." She noticed the expressive lines around his mouth, the aging process that had altered his features, cutting masculine grooves into his skin.

He reminded her of a model in a cowboy ad. The stereotyped Texan, with his hard-angled cheekbones, slightly crooked nose and lightly peppered jaw. But she knew he was real.

Tangible. Touchable. Flesh and blood.

Even after all these years she still wondered what it would feel like to kiss him.

When she lifted her gaze to his, he dipped his hat even lower, shielding his eyes.

Just like old times, she thought. She'd never been able to break through Ethan's defenses. Even though he'd been attracted to her, he'd kept his distance, making her long for him even more.

Not that she would let herself long for him now. Kissing him, or even fantasizing about it, would be a mistake.

"You must be working today," she said, trying to resume a casual conversation.

"Yes, I am. But I live here, too."

She started. "On the Double Crown?"

"It's only temporary. I'm in between homes right now, so I'm renting the hunting cabin from Ryan." He gestured to the barn. "Of course I'm boarding my horses here, too."

From what she recalled, Ethan had been living on the rough-and-tumble property his father owned. Although she wondered why he was moving, she decided not to ask, not to delve too deeply into his affairs, even if she wanted to, even if everything about him still intrigued her. "I've never been inside the hunting cabin."

"Really?" He shifted his feet, scattering dirt beneath his heels. "There isn't much to see, but you can come by later if you want to."

Surprised by the invitation, Susan didn't know what to say. He'd never asked her to visit him before. He'd never encouraged her advances. Of course, this time she wasn't falling all over him. At least not outwardly. Inside, her heart was skipping girlish beats.

"Thanks," she finally managed.

"Sure."

While silence stretched between them, the wind kicked up, the scent of hay and horses triggering her senses. In the distance cattle grazed, like colored dots on the horizon.

"I better go," he said. "I have an appointment on another ranch."

She told herself to relax, to not make a big deal out of his offer. "It was nice talking to you, Ethan."

"You, too," he told her.

He climbed behind the wheel of his white dually, and she watched him start the engine. Within no time, he was gone.

The boy with the slow, sexy smile.

She returned to the house and headed for the kitchen, where she found Lily, bustling around the stove.

Susan stood in the doorway, admiring the woman Ryan had married. Even at fifty-nine, Lily had the power to turn heads. Long limbed and voluptuous, she wore a mint-colored sweater and a loose skirt, attire that was as unpretentious as her style. Her midnight hair was fastened into a simple twist, leaving the angles of her face unframed.

"That smells good," Susan said, indicating the pot of broth simmering on the stove.

Lily looked up, her large, exotic-shaped eyes radiating warmth. "It's corn soup. An old Apache recipe."

Which made sense, considering Lily was part Apache and part Spanish.

Susan moved farther into the kitchen and watched as Lily mixed several pounds of boiled, shredded beef with a homemade batch of acorn meal. She suspected that Lily had taken her time, peeling the acorns and grinding them, a task that was meant to keep her mind off Ryan's illness, especially on this gloomy morning.

A second later Lily took a shaky breath, then glanced out the window as though someone were stalking her. And why not? Susan knew that a man named Jason Jamison, a cold-blooded killer, had been threatening the family. Of course Ryan had hired a security team to protect them. He wouldn't leave something like that to chance.

"Are you okay?" she asked Lily.

"I'm fine. Just jittery, that's all. There's so much to deal with right now." She turned away from the window. "Will you check on Ryan? And if he's awake, will you tell him that I'll bring him some soup later?"

"Sure. But if you need someone to talk to, I'm here."

"I know." Lily gave her a brave smile. "I'm glad you're staying with us. I like having you around."

Her heart bumped her chest, filling her with a sense of longing, of family, of home and hearth. Lily hadn't been Ryan's wife when Susan had lived on the Double Crown, but she'd gotten to know her later. Mostly from trips Ryan and Lily had taken to San Francisco, where they'd traveled to visit her.

"Thank you," Susan told her. "That means a lot to me."

Lily nodded, and they simply gazed at each other, caught in a soundless moment.

After the older woman resumed her task, adding the beef and acorn meal to the broth, Susan left the kitchen, her emotions tugging at her sleeve.

She walked through the great room, her boots echoing on tiled floors, as restless as the Fortune empire ghosts.

Over the years, the house, a traditional adobe structure, had undergone quite a few renovations. At one point it had been divided into two separate wings, where Ryan and his older brother, Cameron, lived with their families. But Susan knew that Cameron had died over ten years ago, leaving Ryan to pick up the pieces of his brother's lazy yet tremulous life.

She headed to Ryan and Lily's room, a master suite with a private bathroom, hot tub and sauna. The door leading to the sitting area was open, a sign that her cousin was awake. She knocked anyway, a light tap to announce her presence.

"Come in," he called out.

She entered the room and saw him sitting on a small sofa near the fireplace. To Susan, Ryan had always seemed larger than life, an invincible force with his solid frame and darkly handsome features. But an inoperable brain tumor had challenged his strength, creating symptoms he could no longer hide.

"How are you feeling?" she asked.

"Better now that you're here."

He patted the cushion next to him, and she moved forward. He didn't look particularly refreshed from his nap, but she was grateful that he was coherent. Earlier, he'd been too dizzy to converse with her.

She sat down and took his hand, holding it gently in hers. "I love you."

A smile wobbled his mouth. "I love you, too, little girl."

"I'm not little anymore."

He gave her hand a light squeeze. "You're still my baby."

She wanted to ask him about Jason Jamison, to discuss the details, but she didn't want to alert him that his beloved wife was fretting in the kitchen, looking over her shoulder every chance she got. Sooner or later Susan would learn everything there was to know about Jason. Both of her brothers had warned her about this man, suggesting that she talk to Ryan about him. Which she intended to do, just not now.

"Lily's making soup," she said, trying to sound more cheerful than she felt.

"What kind?"

"Apache corn. She's going to bring you some when it's done."

"That sounds good." He released her hand. "What did you do today?"

"I went for a walk. Down by the barn." She studied the fireplace, the rugged structure, the natural beauty of each carefully placed stone. "I ran into Ethan."

"Really?" Ryan perked up. "How'd it go?"

"Fine. We only talked for a few minutes." She glanced at her cousin and saw him scrutinizing her beneath his dark brows. Anxious, she fidgeted, then caught herself, folding her hands on her lap. "I used to have a crush on him."

"I know you did, pumpkin. I think everyone knew."

Embarrassed, she laughed a little, picturing herself as she was, a teenager in tight clothes and too much mascara. "I wasn't very subtle about it."

"It's hard to hide those kinds of feelings." He was still watching her, looking at her with a knowing expression. "Old crushes run deep." He paused, then said, "Lily was the love of my life when I was young. And look what happened to us."

She shook her head. "It's not like that between Ethan and me. I hardly know him."

"The heart doesn't forget."

She leaned forward, tempted to touch Ryan's cheek. She knew he'd loved his first wife. She'd been his childhood friend, the woman who bore his children. But Lily was the fire in his soul. "You're just an old romantic."

"And you're a young woman who needs a good man."

"I have my career."

"And a big, empty condo in California. That's not enough, Susan."

"I'm not ready to fall in love." And especially not with Ethan, she decided. She didn't need the complication. Not now. Not while she was in Texas. "I spent enough time mooning over him."

"Like I used to do over Lily?"

She leaned back against the sofa, doing her damnedest not to lose the fight. Apparently Ryan was determined to drive his point home, to compare his life to hers. "I never pegged you for a matchmaker."

"Are you kidding? Me? The old romantic?" He chuckled under his breath. "It's right up my alley."

She forced a smile, humoring him. And humoring herself, as well.

Because deep down, she wanted to see Ethan

again, to summon the courage to stop by the hunting cabin. But she knew she wouldn't.

Susan wasn't about to chase him.

Not ever again.

Chapter 2

Ethan parked his truck and entered the outer courtyard of the main house, where native plants and ornamental grasses flourished. He took the stone walkway, wondering if he was doing the right thing. Dusk had long since fallen and Susan hadn't showed up at his place. For some self-absorbed reason, he'd expected her to visit him, to take advantage of his invitation. Seventeen years ago, she would've jumped at the chance.

But apparently times had changed.

He blew out a rough breath and inhaled the night-blooming flowers that flanked his path. Was it too late to call on her?

He adjusted his hat, lowering it on his head. Susan never failed to make his blood warm, even when they were kids. He had no business wanting her. Not then and not now.

But he couldn't help it.

When they were teenagers, he'd heard all sorts of stories about her. He had no idea if the rumors were true. According to gossip, she'd slept with a slew of boys in Red Rock. She'd supposedly de-virginized a few of them, too.

Not that his fantasies hadn't run in that direction. She'd been the object of every wet dream he could remember. But he'd had other dreams about her, too. He'd wanted to protect her, to heal her the way he'd learned to minister to the animals on the ranch. But Susan hadn't been a wounded filly or an ailing calf. She'd been wild and independent, as raw as the confusion she'd caused.

The confusion she was still causing.

Ethan wanted to give in to temptation. He wanted to unlock the mystery of the girl he'd refrained from touching, the girl who'd bloomed into a sophisticated woman.

With anxiety churning in his gut, he mounted the front steps. Why hadn't she stopped by the hunting cabin to see him? Had she deliberately left him panting after her? Or was he reading too much into it?

Either way, he was trapped, locked in good and tight.

The way she used to flirt with him. The nights he'd spent thinking about her. Every last memory was magnified in his mind, right down to the day she'd gone off to college.

The day she'd disappeared from his life.

Ethan cleared his thoughts, then knocked on the door, expecting Lily to answer his summons. But when Susan appeared, wearing a flowing robe draped over a pair of silky pajamas, he wished he'd had the sense to forget about her.

She presented a soft, sultry image, with the top button on her pajamas straining above her breasts. The robe gaped in that spot, drawing his gaze to the slight swell of cleavage.

"Ethan?"

He pulled his gaze to her face. Her honey-blond hair fell in a loose, nighttime style, lightly combed and framing her chin. He wondered if it smelled like lemons. Her hair had been longer when they were younger, and the citrus scent used to drive him half-mad. Not that she would know the difference. He'd never mentioned it.

"I wasn't expecting you." She tightened the belt on her robe, but her modest effort didn't change a thing.

He could still see the straining button.

He cleared his throat. "I hope it's not too late for a visit."

"No. Of course not." She recovered her composure. "Ryan and Lily already went to bed, but I was just getting ready to fix a cup of tea. Would you like some?"

He rarely drank tea, but he wasn't about to turn her down, not after showing up at her door. "Sure. That'd be nice."

Ethan followed her into the kitchen, where she filled a stainless steel kettle, the kind that whistled, and set it on the stove. He remembered that his mom used to boil water in one of those. As a child, he used to wonder what made it cry out.

When Susan turned to look at him, he caught himself frowning.

"Are you okay?" she asked.

He wiped the surly expression off his face. Thinking about his mom always put him in a bad mood. "I'm fine."

She invited him to sit in the dining room, where she was still close enough to hear the whistle blow.

He removed his denim jacket and placed it over the back of a chair. But he didn't expect her to remove her robe. She still had it cinched. As a teenager, she used to show a lot of flesh, wearing skimpy outfits designed to set his gender on fire. Yet somehow, the misbehaving button on her pajama top seemed even sexier than all those cropped T-shirts and short-shorts ever did.

"Is there something special you wanted to talk to me about?" she asked.

Suddenly Ethan had the urge to bolt. He didn't know what to say, how to explain his compulsion to see her at this hour, so he faked it the best he could. "We didn't have much time to visit earlier, to catch up on old times."

She smoothed the Aztec-printed placemat in front of her. "You had an appointment."

"I'm not in a hurry now." Which was a lie, of course. He was anxious as hell, impatient to cross the finish line, to have a zipper-blasting affair with her. He'd always been sexually obsessed with her, but things had been complicated when they were young.

She tilted her head. "So that's your only agenda? To catch up on old times?"

Guilt clawed at his chest. She'd come home to be with Ryan, to help him face the prospect of death. Tearing up the sheets with a man from her past didn't factor into the equation. "You think I have ulterior motives? Me? The guy who never even kissed you?"

Susan appeared to be pondering his words. And worse yet, she was assessing his body language. He could tell by the way she looked at him. He wondered if she could see through him, if that was part of her job, something psychologists of her caliber were able to do.

"You didn't come here tonight to see how much I've changed? To decide if I'm still a bad girl deep inside?"

He cursed beneath his breath, wishing he'd stayed away from her. "I came here because—"

The whistle on the kettle blew, nearly jarring him out of his skin. She hopped up, bumping the table, rattling his emotions.

"I'll go get our tea," she said.

He waited in the dining room. Once the kettle stopped making noise, the house fell into a slumberous hush. Nothing stirred but his heart.

Trying to relax, Ethan looked around. The Spanish-style decor appealed to him. He liked the heavy woods and rich textures.

Susan returned with a clay-colored tray that held two stoneware cups, a small variety of tea bags, a bowl of sugar and a cow-shaped creamer.

He chose an herbal blend that came in an orange packet, but he didn't add anything to it. Susan picked the same flavor, doctoring hers with sugar and milk.

The drink was warm against his throat, more soothing than he expected. And he was glad she'd provided sturdy cups. His hands were too big for delicate china.

"Go ahead and finish what you were going

to say," she told him. "Tell me why you're really here."

He opted for honesty. But not *complete* honesty. He was keeping his hunger to himself. "It bugged me that you didn't stop by today."

"I considered it. But I didn't want you to think I was starting that old cycle again. Throwing myself at you."

Her admission gave him a boost of confidence. "Maybe we could do something together. Go on a date or something."

"A date?" She sounded intrigued yet wary, still unsure of his intentions.

He backed off a bit, lifting one shoulder in an easy shrug. "Just something casual."

She sucked in a breath. "Like what?"

"We could go for a ride tomorrow afternoon. It's supposed to warm up." And he was willing to rearrange his schedule to spend some time with her. "Around noon?"

"Do you have a horse that would suit me? I never was a skilled rider."

"I've got a gentle old mare. I inherited her from one of my clients. I got roped into some dogs, too. And there's a wild squirrel that pesters me for attention."

She gave him a sweet smile. "You were always good with strays. With the wild ones, too."

Grateful, he returned her smile. He'd always

considered her a stray. And she'd been as wild as they come. "We can have a picnic. I can pick up some deli food."

"Why don't you let me pack our lunch? It will be my contribution to the date."

"Thanks. That sounds great. I'll trailer the horses to the hunting cabin ahead of time. You can meet me there instead of the barn."

She agreed, and he finished his tea and left before it got too late. But as they said goodbye, they parted without any physical contact. No hug, no kiss on the cheek.

Nothing that indicated what tomorrow would bring.

The following morning a puffy blue sky presided over leafy plants and flowering perennials. Susan shared the inner courtyard with Lily and Ryan, who sat across from her at a glass-topped table. This was Susan's favorite place on the Double Crown. An old-fashioned swing was positioned beneath a vine-draped arbor, and a fountain bubbled in the morning air.

Breakfast consisted of a Spanish omelet, buttered toast, orange juice and coffee. Ryan added more salsa to his omelet, and Susan was glad to see him up and about, enjoying quality time with his wife.

"You look pretty this morning," Lily said to Susan.

"Thank you." Susan was dressed in a red T-shirt and Wrangler jeans. Her boots, a sorrel shade of brown, sported a heart design on the toes. She'd fussed over her appearance, taking extra care with her hair and makeup. She'd tried to create a natural look, something that suited her outdoor date with Ethan.

Ryan squinted at Susan, the lines around his eyes crinkling his tanned skin. "You don't seem very hungry."

She glanced up from her plate. "I usually eat a light breakfast. Besides, I'm going on a picnic with Ethan, and I'm trying to save room."

The older man smiled. "Well, that didn't take long, did it? You've only been here for one day and you two made plans already."

"Don't tease me. I'm already nervous." She checked her watch. "I've been up since the crack of dawn." And now she still had two hours to go. But she'd already fried a batch of chicken and filled a plastic container with homemade potato salad.

Ryan's smile shifted to his wife. "We decided to sleep in. To cozy up a bit."

A girlish blush stained Lily's cheeks, and Susan wondered what it would feel like to have a husband, to turn off the alarm clock and snuggle in a pair of strong arms, to know he would always be there.

No, she thought, her emotions turning sad. He wouldn't *always* be there. If marriage didn't end in divorce, then it ended in death.

There was no pain-free escape.

"Tell me about Jason Jamison," she said, her mind drifting to the criminal who'd been haunting her family.

Ryan set down his fork. "He's a madman. A disgruntled relative."

"He's one of us?"

"In a roundabout way. As you know, my father, Kingston, was adopted by the Fortune family. And a man named Travis Jamison was his biological father."

"And Jason is a descendent of Travis?"

Ryan nodded, but Lily didn't move. She sat quietly, listening to Susan and her husband discuss the Fortune legacy.

"Did Travis know about Kingston?" Susan asked. "Did he know he had a son?"

"No. But once Jason discovered that he was a long-lost relative of my father, he swooped down on us like the vulture he is."

Lily finally spoke. "Jason is a killer. A heartless murderer."

A chill rattled Susan's spine, like ice chips scraping against each and every vertebra. She already knew that Jason was a killer, but hearing Lily say it, listening to the anxiety in her voice, brought the reality that much closer to home.

"Did Vincent tell you that Natalie witnessed one of the murders?" Lily asked.

Susan nodded. Vincent was her oldest brother and he'd filled her in about what Natalie, his new bride, had seen. "Jason strangled his own lover. A woman he was passing off as his wife."

"That's right," Lily said. "And before that, Jason shot his own brother."

Susan couldn't imagine someone killing his or her sibling. But according to the Bible, Cain had slain Abel. It wasn't something new.

"Jason has another brother," Ryan put in. "And this one's an FBI agent. He's going to contact me when he gets into town. He's put other killers behind bars, and he's not going to rest until he catches Jason."

"What's his name?" Susan asked, curious about the man Ryan was putting his faith in.

"Emmett," he told her. "Emmett Jamison."

"Jason already escaped from prison," Lily told Susan. "It happened while he was being transferred to a maximum-security facility." She paused, took a breath. "We're grateful that Special Agent Jamison is on his tail. We need all the help we can get."

Ryan took his wife's hand. "It will be okay, honey. I promise, it will."

"I know. But I couldn't bear it if he hurt someone in our family." She met Susan's gaze across the table. "Just because we have security on the ranch doesn't mean that you shouldn't be careful. Or take their presence for granted."

Ryan interjected. "Of course she'll be careful. We all will. But we can't live in fear. We can't let Jason destroy our lives." He brought Lily's hand to his lips and brushed a kiss across her knuckles. "We deserve some happiness. Some peace and quiet."

Susan didn't say anything. She let Ryan give his wife the comfort she needed. The support only a husband, the man who loved her, could provide.

At noon, Susan arrived at the hunting cabin. She parked the SUV she'd borrowed from Ryan behind Ethan's truck and trailer and noticed the horses that were tied to a hitching post on the side of the property.

The building itself, a rustic log structure, sat on a piece of land that blended into the horizon, stretching as far as the eye could see. In the front yard a scatter of trees provided shady ambience, and a rough-hewn porch offered two sturdy, old barrel chairs, where a trio of dogs enjoyed the afternoon sun.

The largest of the three, a black Lab, lifted its head as Susan approached, then leaped forward to greet her like an old friend. The other two, mutts of unknown origin, barely paid her any mind.

Within seconds, Ethan flung open the door, and her pulse jumped to her throat. He looked tall and strong—a man with a powerful presence. Shadows cut across his shoulders, dappling the front of a chambray shirt. Beneath the brim of his ever-present hat, those bright blue eyes glittered like twin jewels.

The mixed-breed dogs glanced up at him, but the Lab stayed by her side.

"He likes women," Ethan told her.

"So you're a boy," she said to the Lab.

"His name is Chocolate. But don't blame me for that. My ex-girlfriend named him."

Curious, Susan tilted her chin. His voice held no malice, but it didn't ring of affection, either, or any kind of substantial loss. It made her wonder about Ethan's capacity to fall in love.

"Are you analyzing me?" he asked.

Caught red-handed, she adjusted the canvas bag over her shoulder. "What can I say? You're a fascinating subject. Besides, you brought up your ex."

"Only because of Chocolate's name. And you fascinate me, too. You always did. Even if I never kissed you."

Susan glanced at his mouth, and that familiar

smile spread across his lips. He was flirting with her, letting down his guard. And she was tempted to flirt back, to enjoy the affection she used to crave from him.

Enraptured, they gazed at each other, with Chocolate standing between them. Then the dog decided he wanted some attention and jammed his nose against Susan's crotch.

She started, and Ethan bit back a laugh.

"I told you he liked women."

"That's not funny. You should correct him."

"I do, but he never listens. Especially about that."

"So you just gave up?"

He shrugged, and she shook her head and shoved the canvas bag at him. A gentle shove that had him smiling at her again.

"What's in here?" he asked. "Dirty magazines? A month's supply of condoms?"

She raised her eyebrows. When Ethan flirted, he *flirted*. No holds barred. "It's our lunch, you pervert."

"Look who's talking. The girl who drove every boy in the county mad."

"I don't do that anymore."

"Wanna bet?" He grinned and peered into the bag, examining the contents. "Fried chicken gets a guy every time."

"There are cookies in there, too."

"Chocolate chip?"

She glanced at the Lab, making sure he didn't react too strongly to his name. "Peanut butter. But I didn't bake them. They were left over in the kitchen."

"I'll bet Rosita made them," he said, referring to Ryan and Lily's housekeeper. "She used to give me sweets when I was a kid."

Susan nodded. She knew that Rosita's husband, Ruben, was a retired ranch hand, a man who'd worked with Ethan's dad. "How's your father doing these days?" she asked, assuming he'd retired, as well.

Ethan's easy manner faltered. "Dad died four months ago. I guess Ryan didn't tell you."

"No, he didn't. I'm sorry."

"Ryan's had a lot on his mind." He heaved a heavy sigh. "But he took it pretty hard. He and Dad were close."

"So were you and your father," she said, recalling the stable relationship they'd had, the respect between them. "I always envied you that."

"It's been tough these past few months. I really miss him." He closed the canvas bag, shifting his gaze, changing the subject. "Why don't you come in and see the cabin? Then we can go for a ride and eat all the wonderful food you brought."

She followed him into the house, with Chocolate nipping at her heels. The other dogs remained outside.

The cabin consisted of one large room, a simple kitchen and a closet-size bathroom. Animal pelts and hunting trophies lined the walls. A leather couch that she assumed was a sofa bed sat adjacent to a stone fireplace, and braided area rugs padded portions of the wood floor. In the corner, a small oak table accommodated two rustic chairs.

"None of this stuff is mine," Ethan said. "My belongings are in storage. I'm waiting for escrow to close on the gentleman's ranch I bought."

"Gentleman's ranch?"

"A property with less than a hundred acres," he explained. "Where the owner makes his living at something other than ranching."

"Did you sell your dad's house after he died?"

Ethan nodded. "He'd already signed the deed over to me. But I just couldn't live there anymore. Too many memories. I figured this was a good time to start over. But the escrow dates didn't mesh, so that's why I'm in between homes, renting this place from Ryan."

"I live in a condo near the wharf," she offered.

He searched her gaze. "Do you like San Francisco?"

As a montage of overworked days and exhausted nights spun through her mind, she contemplated her answer. "I fit in there."

He pushed his hat back a little, revealing the expression in his eyes. An emotion she couldn't quite name.

"You're a city girl," he said.

"I'm dressed like a country girl today. Wranglers instead of designer jeans."

Her comment made him smile, but only for a moment. His intensity remained. She couldn't think of anything to say, so she let the silence engulf them. Ethan had been a complicated boy, and he'd grown into a complex man. But she expected as much.

"Should we saddle the horses?" she finally asked.

"Sure." He was still holding the food she'd prepared. "Country boys like me need to get out on the open range."

"Sounds okay to me," she teased. "I've always had a thing for you cowboy types."

"I know." He angled his head to look at her, to roam his gaze over her body. "Opposites attract. It's a trick of nature. What gets us in trouble."

Heat spiraled through her veins, making her sexually aware, reminding her of how long it had been since she'd had a lover, a man who meant something to her. But even so, Susan knew better. "We're not in trouble."

"Yes, we are," he said, as he took her hand and led her outside, making her pulse pound all over again.

Chapter 3

"Just because we're attracted to each other doesn't mean something is going to happen," Susan said.

Ethan eyed his companion. They stood beside the hitching post, the sun glaring above their heads, raining warmth down their backs. Whom was she trying to convince? Him or herself? "If you say so."

"I do." She struggled with the girth. "Nothing happened when we were kids and nothing is going to happen now."

He took over, nudging her aside, realizing she

didn't remember how to saddle a horse. "Nothing happened because I didn't let it."

"And I'm not going to let it happen this time," she said.

He shrugged, told himself it didn't matter. "I'm okay with just being friends."

"So am I." She turned to look at him, to ease the tension, to create a casual vibe.

But it didn't work. Not for Ethan. He wanted to touch her, to smooth her hair away from her cheek, to brush his mouth across hers.

Friendship had its drawbacks, he thought.

He finished saddling their horses, then packed their picnic supplies.

"What's my mare's name?" she asked.

"Serene."

"That's a calm name."

"She's a calm horse. But she's lazy, too." He patted the old Appaloosa's neck. "Of course, she plods along just fine on trail. She'll follow Sequoia anywhere."

"Sequoia." Susan studied his gelding. "That fits him. He's nearly as big as a redwood tree. The same color, too." She leaned against the hitching post. "We have lots of redwoods in California."

"I've never been there." He wouldn't mind taking a trip to the Sequoia National Forest, but that was as far as his interest in California went. He couldn't imagine himself in Susan's neck of the woods, traipsing around San Francisco like a misplaced cowboy.

She moved closer to Serene, letting the horse get to know her. Ethan watched her fuss with the mare's mane, combing her fingers through it. Serene seemed pleased, but he figured the Appaloosa recognized a sucker when she saw one. Susan was babying her as if she were a child.

He squinted beneath the brim of his hat. "You're spoiling her."

"She's already spoiled."

"She came that way."

Susan stroked Serene's nose. "Oh, that's right. You inherited her from one of your clients." She bumped his shoulder, teasing him. "And now you're stuck with her."

"She needed a home. And Sequoia bonded with her." He bumped Susan's shoulder right back. "Do you need a boost up?"

"I can handle it." She grabbed the horn and hoisted herself onto the mare's back, the saddle creaking beneath her butt.

Ethan adjusted her stirrups. "How's that?"

"Good." She pushed her heels down. "I'm glad you invited me on a date. It's nice to spend some time with you."

"I think so, too." He liked the changes in her, but he liked remembering her as she'd been, too.

The girl he'd wanted to protect. The girl who'd needed someone to care.

Ready to hit the trail, he mounted his horse, wishing she'd give him a chance. He didn't understand what harm would come from a romantic interlude, from a man and woman, two consenting adults, exploring the chemistry that had always been between them.

Chocolate wagged his tail and barked.

"You're not coming with us," Ethan told him.

The dog barked again, only louder this time. Then he whined and looked at Susan.

"Why can't he come?" she asked.

"Because he's a pest."

"I don't mind."

"So you say. Just wait."

"We can't leave him here. Not like that." By now, the Lab was practically pleading, howling like the con artist he was.

Most veterinarians owned animals that behaved. But not Ethan. He adopted every stubborn creature that came his way. "He's going to try to mooch off our plates."

"I'll fix him his own plate."

"That won't pacify him, but I'm game if you are." He started down the trail. Susan took the spot next to him, with Chocolate padding confidently beside her.

They rode on a sun-dappled path, their horses

moving at a relaxed pace. The sky was the color of a robin's egg, and the ground offered shades of brown and green. Most of the area was flat and clear, but in the distance, live oaks dotted the terrain like Texas-bred sentries. Farther out, a grouping of hills made a regal statement. Ethan loved this land. To him, it represented God's country, a place where the world stopped to sigh.

Rabbits darted past, making Chocolate perk his ears. But the dog didn't leave Susan's side.

They headed for the live oaks, where they decided to have their picnic.

The path they traveled narrowed, so Susan fell into step behind Ethan. He could hear Serene's footsteps as she picked her way through the brush.

Once they reached the oaks, the trail opened onto a grassy slope. "How's this?" Ethan asked, stopping beneath an enormous tree, where branches reached across the sky.

"It's perfect."

After they dismounted, he tended to the horses and she spread a blanket on the ground, smoothing it over the bumpy surface.

Chocolate danced in canine delight, sniffing the air in anticipation, waiting for the foodfest to begin.

Susan looked up at Ethan. "Did you raise him from a pup?"

He glanced at the dog and the silly beast had

the gall to grin. "No. I've only had him about six months. He was homeless and hanging out behind Red, the Mexican restaurant in town, begging for burritos and whatnot. The owner felt bad for him, but he was making a nuisance of himself, barking at the back door all the time. My girlfriend, Amber, was a waitress there, so she brought him to me."

She patted the pooch's head. "And you had no choice but to keep him?"

"Amber wanted him, but Chocolate was too rambunctious around her son."

She unpacked their lunch. "Your old girlfriend has a child?"

He nodded. "A two-year-old. Truthfully, I miss her little boy more than her. But she reunited with his father, so they're trying to make a stable home for him." He stretched his legs and saw how frayed his jeans were. Susan's, he noticed, were brand spanking new. "It's what she wanted all along. I was her rebound, but I knew that from the beginning."

"No love lost on your part?"

"No. How about you?"

"I've been in two serious relationships, but my career got in the way both times." Her voice turned analytical. "I have a difficult time balancing my work and my love life."

Ethan thought about his mom, then quickly

brushed her aside. He didn't want Susan to know that his mother had chosen her career over her family. Or that his dad had never gotten over her. "I'd like to have a wife and kids someday, but I don't let it consume me. I'm used to being single."

"Me, too. But it gets lonely sometimes."

"Yeah, but it's better than a crappy marriage."

"Amen to that." She fed the dog first, a lunch that he gobbled up in record time, nudging her for more. She obliged, then gave him an apple to play with while she and Ethan filled their paper plates with chicken, fruit and potato salad, keeping the cookies packed and out of Chocolate's reach.

All too soon, the dog got bored with the apple and begged off Susan's plate, just like Ethan knew he would. He'd been trying to break Chocolate of that habit, but he didn't have the heart to scold him. The mutt had forged a cozy spot for himself, resting his head in her lap.

"You're a bottomless pit." She fed Chocolate more chicken, and he licked his chops.

"I can hardly blame him," Ethan said. "This is good."

"Thank you." She smiled, making him envy the dog.

She looked pretty in the afternoon light, with her honey-colored hair and green eyes. Chic and sophisticated, even in jeans and boots and her lipstick wearing off.

He glanced at her mouth and wondered if she would let him kiss her when their date ended. Or would that be crossing the friendship line?

"Our timing is off," he heard himself say.

"Why? Because I don't sleep around anymore?"

"I didn't mean it like that." He removed bottled water from the saddlebag and took a swig. "I'm impressed with the way you grew up, but I miss you having a crush on me."

She set her half-empty plate on the blanket. Chocolate was no longer interested in her food. He'd fallen asleep in her lap. "It wasn't a healthy crush. Nothing I did then was healthy."

Ethan drank more water, but he wasn't able to cool his heels. "So now you're tempering your feelings for me?"

"I can't go back in time. I can't become the old Susan, the girl who acted out her pain."

He longed to touch her, to glide his fingers along her jaw, to comfort the girl she used to be. "I don't want to go back in time, either. Can't we separate the past from the present? Start over somehow?"

"I don't know. Can we? I'll bet you haven't forgotten any of those rumors. I'll bet they're still occupying your mind."

"Can you blame me?" He looked up and saw a hawk dive from a tree branch and sail into the air, like a red-tipped angel taking flight. "You were so sweet, so vulnerable, but you were wild, too. It drove me crazy."

"I was trying to fill the void inside me. The emptiness that wouldn't go away."

"I knew you were mixed-up, and I wanted to make everything better. But I didn't know how."

She released a deep, emotional breath, stirring the dog, making him open his eyes for a second. "It wasn't your job to fix me."

Maybe not, but he was paying the price now. She'd fixed herself, and he was left with nothing but his memories. "I wanted to pound the crap out of every boy who touched you," he said. "But there were too many names being bandied around. I never knew what to believe."

"I didn't have as many lovers as everyone said. The rumors got blown out of proportion."

"I was so damn jealous, especially when I heard that you were helping some of those guys lose their virginity."

A mild breeze rustled the leaves above their heads, intensifying the moment. He couldn't help it. He was still jealous, still primed for a war party. But he knew she wasn't going to name names.

"There was only one boy who was a virgin," she finally said. "But at the time, so was I."

Ethan frowned. "Then how did that rumor get started?"

"Because I pretended that I'd done it before. He

was really drunk, so he didn't know the difference." She bit the inside of her lip, as if the experience was still raw. "I knew he would talk about it afterward, and I wanted you to find out."

A lump formed in his throat. "Why? So I'd say 'to hell with it' and lose my virginity to you, too?"

She nodded. "It was the only thing I could think of to get your attention. Nothing else was working."

"I'm sorry, Susan."

"It wasn't your fault. It was me. I did it to myself."

And she'd kept doing it, he thought. She'd kept flaunting other guys in front of him.

Silent, he finished his food and set his plate next to hers, trying to maintain his composure, to ease the sudden tension, the confession in her eyes, the ache in his chest.

"Don't feel guilty, Ethan. Sleeping with that boy didn't change who I was. I'd already been messing around before I came to Red Rock." She gnawed on the inside of her lip again. "Sneaking out of the house, drinking with my friends, learning how to give oral sex."

"I wasn't running wild," he admitted. "But I had a girlfriend before I met you, and we used to engage in some serious foreplay. We just didn't go all the way."

She managed a smile. "And here I thought you were a Boy Scout. Proper Ethan."

"Oh, yeah? Well, you were full of surprises, too. You hardly ever studied, but you got amazing grades. Like a computer nerd or something."

"Being an honor-roll student was easy for me. But being smart wasn't what I was after. Not until I straightened up my life and went off to college."

"Stanford," he said, then let out a low whistle. "You can't beat that."

"Ryan paid for it. I owe him my education."

Ethan had attended Texas A&M, and he'd been strapped with student loans, debts he'd finally paid off. "I tried not to think about you over the years, but I always wondered how you were."

She stroked the top of Chocolate's head, making the big dopey dog sigh in his sleep. "Me, too. Every so often, I'd ask Ryan about you. But I didn't want to overdo it."

"And now here we are. On our first date." He packed up the picnic supplies. "I guess it wasn't as casual as I promised."

She looked around. "The atmosphere was casual."

"But not the conversation."

"Friends should be candid with each other. I'm glad we talked about it."

He raised his eyebrows at her. "You wanna tell my libido that?"

She shrugged, laughed, made a silly face at

him. "You'll get over it. Besides, abstinence makes the heart grow fonder."

"That's absence, smarty." And his heart was already fond of her. Or was that his hormones? At this point, he couldn't be sure.

She woke up the dog and they rode back to the hunting cabin, silence humming between them. Once they arrived, he unsaddled the horses and she offered to let him keep the leftovers, including the untouched cookies.

As she prepared to leave, he debated his options. He knew a kiss was out of the question, but he wasn't about to settle for a handshake.

He opted for a hug, taking an awkward step toward her, like a teenage boy who was about to trip over his own feet. When he took her in his arms, she put her head on his shoulder.

He buried his nose in her hair and inhaled the faded scent of her shampoo. It was lemon, just like when they were young.

She stepped back and smiled at him, but her eyes were a little glassy. He wondered if the contact had made her warm.

"I'll guess we'll see each other around," she said.

He tried to seem unaffected. "Sure. Anytime."

She walked toward the SUV, and Chocolate trotted after her.

"You can't go home with her," Ethan told the dog.

Chocolate ignored the warning. When Susan opened the driver side, he muscled past her and leaped inside. Then he scooted over, waiting for her to get behind the wheel.

She stood beside the vehicle and laughed. "I guess he made up his mind."

Ethan shook his head. "I'll drag his butt out of there."

"No, it's okay. He can stay with me for a while. I'm sure Ryan and Lily won't mind."

"He'll want to sleep in your bed. But he won't keep you warm. He'll hog the covers."

"With all that fur? I'll take my chances." She climbed into the SUV, started the engine and rolled down the windows. Chocolate curled up on the seat.

Ethan figured there was no point in pushing the issue. If she was willing to babysit his dog, there wasn't much he could do. "Call me if he gives you any trouble. Ryan has my number."

"Thank you. I will."

Her gaze caught his and they stared at each other through the passenger window. Then Chocolate popped up and stuck his head in the way, gloating, no doubt, that he'd gotten the girl.

The one Ethan kept losing.

After watching the eleven o'clock news, Susan curled up with Chocolate. A light burned beside the bed, illuminating the room, casting a white sheen over the book in her hand.

The Lab burrowed deeper beside her. He was more than a blanket hog. His body was pressed so close to hers, he could have been her conjoined twin.

"I can't concentrate," she told him as she closed the novel and placed it on the nightstand.

She couldn't quit thinking about Ethan.

The dog yawned, and she scratched his ears, wondering if his master was in bed. Which wasn't a good sign. If her mind strayed too far in that direction, she would start obsessing about Ethan, letting him consume her, as he did when they were young.

No, she thought. She hadn't earned a Ph.D. in psychology to become her own patient all over again. Been there, done that, she told herself.

Then why not analyze Ethan instead? That wasn't the same as obsessing about him, and she had every right to figure out what he was up to.

Why did he want to sleep with her so badly, especially after dodging her teenage advances? Was it a hard-hitting sexual conquest? A man thinking with his penis? A guy who wished he'd nailed the bad girl all those years ago?

On a primal level, that was a definite possibility, something an adult male might consider. But for an elusive boy who'd wanted to make everything better, to heal her rebellious heart, it seemed out of character.

So maybe he was trying to bandage those old wounds. Not consciously, but deep down, where it counted. Where he'd needed her as much as she'd needed him.

But how could she be sure? Ethan had always kept his feelings to himself. Unlike her, who'd rammed her emotions down everyone else's throats.

A light knock sounded at the door, and Chocolate lifted his head, his sleepy eyes going wide.

"It's me," Lily said through the wood.

"Come in," Susan told her.

The older woman entered, then smiled at the dog, who thumped his tail in a friendly greeting. "I see your companion found a cozy spot."

"More than cozy." Susan scratched his ears again. "He's glued to my side."

"I think Ryan half expected you to bring Ethan home instead."

"I would have." She gave Lily a teasing grin. "If I hadn't changed my wicked ways."

Lily chuckled, then sat in a bentwood rocker that creaked with age. She placed her hands on the curved wood and set the chair into a soft, gliding motion. She wore a cotton nightgown and a chenille robe. Her thick hair was fastened into a single braid.

"Is Ryan asleep?" Susan asked.

"He drifted off hours ago, but I can't seem to settle in."

"Too much on your mind?"

"Ryan keeps telling me that he won't let Jason Jamison hurt anyone in our family, but I can't help but worry. Ryan is ill, and there's a madman threatening us. There's only so much I can take."

"I know. I'm so sorry." Susan moved to the edge of the bed, closer to Lily. "I think Ryan is just as worried as you are, but he's trying to remain strong."

"To prove that he can protect us? Even though he's dying?"

Susan nodded. She'd seen the determination on Ryan's face, and she knew how often he consulted his security team. "I wonder when the FBI agent will contact you. When he'll uncover Jason's whereabouts."

"Soon, I hope. That's what's so creepy. Just knowing Jason is out there." She rubbed her arms, even though she was wrapped in a robe. "Maybe I would feel safer if Ryan wasn't ill. Maybe that's why I'm having such a hard time with this. I'm losing my rock, my stability."

"You haven't lost him yet, Lily. He's still here, asleep down the hall."

The older woman blinked away the tears that

gathered in her eyes. "You're right." She let out a deep sigh. "I love him so much."

"And he loves you."

"Yes, he does. And that's the most comforting feeling in the world." She stood, smiled at Susan and Chocolate. "Thank you. It helps to talk."

"For me, too." She came to her feet and gave Lily a hug. The dog climbed off the bed and tried to nuzzle his way between them, wanting to be part of the embrace.

They stepped back and laughed, giving in to the moment, to the humor the Lab provided.

"He doesn't seem like a stray," Lily said.

"Ethan spoils him. He pretends not to, but he does."

Lily looked up at her. "I can hardly blame him. You better hang on to that one."

But after Lily said good-night and left the room, Susan wasn't sure who "that one" was.

Chocolate. Or the man who'd rescued him.

Chapter 4

In the morning Susan took Chocolate for a walk down by the barn. She told herself it wasn't a ploy to see if Ethan was around. She had no idea if Ethan was even working on the Double Crown today. He had other clients, other ranches that paid for his services.

But even so, she scanned the distance, wondering if he was working with the cattle, the animals that looked like irregular-shape dots grazing on the vast Texas land.

Not that it mattered if he was out there somewhere, restraining cows in a chute. She wasn't searching for Ethan, she reminded herself. She was simply taking his dog out to play.

And play Chocolate did. He ran all over the place, disappearing from sight, then returning with sticks and rocks and other makeshift toys in his mouth.

At her feet he dropped a soda can he'd found, then took off again. He hadn't gotten the concept of fetch. He didn't wait around for her to throw his prizes so he could retrieve them. Not that she would toss an aluminum can. She picked it up, intending to throw it away, wondering who'd littered the ranch. She couldn't imagine any of Ryan's employees being that disrespectful, but someone had discarded it.

She heard Chocolate barking and hoped he wasn't getting into any trouble. It appeared to be a playful sound, but he might be bugging one of the ranch hands.

Susan followed the bark and found him behind an outbuilding, along with a teenage girl who sat on the ground, puffing on a cigarette. She looked at Susan without saying a word.

Déjà vu hit her hard and quick.

She saw a reflection of her former self. Not in the girl's appearance, but in the unaffected stare. Susan never flinched when strangers used to catch her smoking, but she remembered how her heart would pound, how she would pray that her dad wouldn't find out.

"Do you know if there's a trash can nearby?" she asked, keeping her tone easy. She wanted to get her point across without backing the child into a corner. She suspected the littered can had come from her.

The teenager shrugged. She wore a nondescript T-shirt, tomboyish jeans and tennis shoes. Strands of wavy brown hair escaped from a simple ponytail. A sprinkling of freckles across her upturned nose gave her face a pixielike quality and so did her petite frame. She appeared to be about fourteen or fifteen. Beside her was a blue-and-yellow backpack.

"Maybe in the barn?" Susan said, referring to the trash can again.

The teen's brown eyes barely blinked. "I suppose."

"I guess I'll throw this away later." For now she decided to introduce herself. "I'm Susan Fortune, Ryan and Lily's cousin. And he's Chocolate," she added as the dog sniffed the girl's jeans.

"I know who he is. The vet's pesky dog."

Susan couldn't help but smile. "He means well. What's your name?"

"Cathy."

She sat down in the dirt, close enough to make

direct eye contact, but not close enough to invade the girl's space. "How well do you know Ethan?"

"My mom used to babysit for his girlfriend's kid when they went out." Cathy squinted at her. "Are you his new girlfriend?"

"No. We're just friends. We knew each other when we were young."

"You kind of look like Amber."

"Really?" Susan recognized the name of Ethan's ex. "How so?"

"I don't know. You just do." A strong pull on the cigarette filled her lungs. "Except she's prettier than you."

Ouch, Susan thought. This kid knew how to pack a punch. It made her wonder what or whom Cathy was lashing out at. "Do you go to school around here?"

"Where else would I go? I live on the ranch."

"You're a long way from the bus stop. Shouldn't you get going?" Susan decided to up the ante, to use a little friendly force. "Or are you planning to ditch?"

"I was just getting ready to leave." Cathy stood, stamped out her cigarette and left it on the ground. Then she grabbed her backpack and took off, disappearing around the corner of the building.

Chocolate barked, and Susan sighed and went after the cigarette butt, dropping it inside the empty can. She had enough problems to contend

with; she didn't need to worry about one more try-
ing-to-be-tough teen. The world was filled with
rebellious youths, and she couldn't help them all.

But Cathy lived on the Double Crown and that
made Susan think that fate had intervened. That
she should explore Cathy's situation, at least ask
Ethan about her.

Susan waited until dusk to show up at Ethan's
door. He answered her knock with his hair damp
and his chest bare. A pair of jeans rode haphaz-
ardly on his hips.

He'd just taken a shower, she realized. And
climbed into his pants. His fly wasn't open, but
several teeth on his zipper were exposed, drawing
her gaze below his belly button.

"Are you here to return my dog?"

"What? No." She looked up and felt her cheeks
sting with bad-girl heat. She shouldn't be examining him like a side of beef. "Chocolate is with
Ryan and Lily."

He glanced over her shoulder. "Are you sure he
didn't follow you?"

"I'm sure. He was napping when I left the
house." Her gaze strayed again. Faded denim, the
waistband of his boxers peeking out. She wanted
to touch him, to put her hands where they didn't
belong.

She meant to tell him that she'd stopped by to

ask him about Cathy, but suddenly she couldn't think beyond his body, beyond his half-naked appeal.

He gestured for her to enter the cabin. She walked inside and took a deep breath.

When he closed the door, she noticed a tattoo on his shoulder. Two horseshoes and a star branding his flesh. "When did you do that?"

He turned to face her. "Do what?"

"The ink."

"Five years ago. For luck, when I turned thirty." He gave her a half-cocked smile. "I'll probably do it again when I turn forty."

"On the other shoulder?"

"I haven't decided." He grabbed a shirt that was draped over the sofa. "Do you have any hidden artwork I should know about?"

"Like a pirate ship on my chest? No, I can't say that I do."

"I was thinking more along the lines of a rose on your thigh." He slipped on the shirt, but didn't button it. A grin slid across his face. "Or maybe a butterfly on your sweet little—"

She raised her eyebrows at him. Ethan Eldridge had turned into a dark and daring man. "You missed your chance to see my butt."

"Don't remind me how stupid I was." He paused and his expression turned serious. "Do you want to have dinner with me tonight?"

The change of topic threw her off-kilter. She blinked, reminding herself that she'd arrived at his house to ask him about Cathy.

"We can go to Red," he said.

Red? The restaurant where his ex-girlfriend worked? "When?"

"In a few minutes. I just have to finish getting dressed."

"Sounds good. I haven't eaten yet." She decided she would ask him about Cathy over dinner. And maybe, if Amber was working, she would get a glimpse of the woman she supposedly resembled.

Even if Amber was prettier.

She sat on the sofa while Ethan got ready. He buttoned his shirt in front of her, but turned his back to unzip his jeans and tuck in his shirttail. A belt came next. She could hear the clank of the buckle.

She didn't think he was as modest as he seemed. He'd probably done it out of respect to her.

Finally, he walked over to an oak armoire and removed a pair of socks from the single drawer. The cabin didn't have a bedroom, and she shifted on the sofa, realizing she was sitting on his bed.

He reached for his boots and sat next to her, pulling them on. His dark brown hair, she noticed, had yet to dry. He wore it short and just a little messy. His temples bore fine threads of gray, barely visible, but still a testament of time, of the years that had passed.

"Don't wear a hat," she said.

He made a face. "Why not?"

"I like how you look without it." And she didn't want him to hide beneath the brim.

He ran a hand through his hair, trying, it seemed, to tame it. But his finger combing didn't make much of a difference. "I feel naked."

But he wasn't, she thought. He was fully clothed now. "I heard that hats make men go bald."

"Then I'd really be naked." He gave his Stetson or Resistol or whatever it was a longing glance. "This bites."

She smiled, knowing she'd won. "Maybe I'll kiss you tonight."

His Adam's apple bobbed. "Really?"

"On the cheek."

"Tease." He stood and offered to help her up.

She accepted his hand and his sense of humor. His eyes were twinkling, as blue as the sea, as the sky, as every poetic description she could think of.

A moment later, they took his truck and left for the restaurant in companionable silence.

Red was a converted two-story hacienda brimming with charm. The first floor served as the eatery, with dark wood tables and terra-cotta tiles. Leafy plants and dim lighting offered a cozy atmosphere.

Susan and Ethan sat at a candle-steeped table, and from her vantage point, Susan could see the courtyard where paper lanterns were strung, like leftover holiday lights bouncing off red umbrellas.

The waitress, a friendly brunette, brought them their menus, took their drink orders and departed with a swish of her flouncing uniform. Susan glanced around. Amber, she assumed, was blond.

"The combination platters are really good," Ethan said.

Susan quit scouting the room and scanned the menu instead. Not a blonde in sight. "Everything looks good."

"Yeah. I'm starving." After a busboy delivered their drinks and placed a basket of chips and a bowl of salsa on the table, Ethan dived into them. "I eat out a lot. It's a hassle to cook for myself."

"For me, too." She pondered over a beef burrito or a chicken enchilada, then gave in to her curiosity. "Did you meet Amber here?"

"Yep." He said it casually, reaching for another chip. "She was separated from her husband and going through a rough time."

"And you helped her?"

"Oh, sure." He laughed a little. "I helped her come to the conclusion that she was still in love with her husband."

Susan dipped into the salsa, waking up her taste buds. "I guess she isn't working tonight."

"Not tonight or any other night. She doesn't work here anymore." He frowned at her. "Did you think I picked this place because of her? I don't play those kinds of games."

"I didn't see it as a game. Besides, I heard that we look alike."

"Who? You and Amber?" He sat back in his chair, the frown digging deeper into his skin. "Who told you that?"

"Cathy."

"Cathy?"

"The teenager whose mom used to babysit Amber's son."

"Oh, *that* Cathy. The kid who sneaks cigarettes. I'll bet she got to you."

"Yes, she did. In fact, she's the reason I came to see you. But first I want to know if what she said is true."

He gave her a point-blank stare. "Why? Is it some sort of crime for me to sleep with petite blondes?"

"So we do look alike."

"Not enough to mix you up. And I didn't even recognize you when I first saw you."

Which meant that Amber looked more like the way she used to look. Longer hair, darker makeup, sexier clothes. "It could be a Freudian crime."

He broke into a smile. "Then you should cure me. Take me to bed or something."

"Nice try." She smiled, too, but her pulse was tripping like an acid-dropping hippie. Even the flame on the candle was jumping.

The waitress came by to take their food order. Suddenly Susan was glad the other woman was a brunette. It was foolish to feel that way, but she couldn't help it. She was getting territorial about Ethan.

By the time their meals arrived, she almost convinced herself that she should sleep with him. Almost. But somewhere in the recesses of her brain, she knew an affair would do spongy things to her heart. In spite of her teenage track record, sex had never been casual. For Susan, it came with a price. An emotional price, where attachments were formed, where she needed her partners to care, even the boys who'd passed her around like candy.

She watched Ethan attack his combination platter. He mixed up his food, the *chili rellenos* and tamales that sat beside hearty helpings of rice and beans.

"Why didn't you kiss me when we were young?" she asked, her thoughts mired in the past. "I knew you wanted to. I could feel it every time we were together."

He nearly dropped his fork. "What kind of question is that?"

"An honest one."

"I didn't want to hurt you. To become part of your pain."

"But the way you looked at me gave me false hope."

"Okay, fine." He frowned, steadied his fork. "You want the whole truth? I wanted to heal you, to sweep you into my world and make you mine. But the idea of losing you scared me. I knew you wouldn't stay in Texas."

Her breath went still; her mind went into its Ph.D. mode. "Who abandoned you, Ethan? Who was I representing?"

"No one. Christ Almighty." He cursed under his breath, then looked up, apologizing, it seemed, to the Man above. "Does everything we do have to be dissected? Analyzed? Chewed up and spit out?"

Guilty as charged, she thought.

"Besides," he went on, "now that we're older, I've been chasing you like a rutting bull. I think that makes us even."

She looked into his eyes and saw his pain, the rejection she was causing. "I'm sorry. But now it's my turn to be afraid. To be wary of an attachment."

"Maybe I can teach you how to get over it." He gave her a gentle smile. "Some things aren't meant to last. Sometimes we have to take life as it comes."

He was right. But he was wrong, too. Sometimes people had to protect their hearts. "I don't have affairs anymore. Not without some sort of commitment."

"Does it have to be a long-term commitment?"

"I like to hope it does. My last two relationships lasted for quite a few years. They didn't work out, but at least I tried."

He lifted his water and took a swig. "Mine never last. But I'm not saying that I won't make a long-term commitment. That it won't ever happen."

She nodded, recalling that he wanted a wife and children someday. "Maybe you're not as detached as you seem."

"Detached? I'm falling at your feet, woman."

"Because you want sex."

"I settled for friendship, didn't I?"

"Yes, you did." And he was turning into a darn good friend, someone she was able to confide in.

"Do you want to talk about Cathy?" he asked. "Dissect her for a while?"

"And take the pressure off of us? Sure." She took a bite of the enchilada she'd barely touched, grateful her appetite was coming back. Cathy was the reason she'd accepted his dinner invitation. Amber, too. But she'd already grilled him about his ex. "Tell me what you know about her."

"She's fourteen, I think. And she's originally from California."

She scooted closer to the table. "Northern California?"

"Southern. The L.A. area. I'm not sure why her family moved to Texas, but they've lived here for about six months. Her dad is a gardener on the ranch. He manages the greenhouse."

"What's he like? What's your assessment of him?"

Ethan continued eating. "He seems like a good guy. Hardworking, easygoing. He's older, though. About Ryan's age."

"And Cathy's mother?"

"She's in her late thirties. A homemaker. She babysits for some of the ranch hands' kids. That's why she used to watch Amber's son when we went out. She came highly recommended."

"Does Cathy have any brothers or sisters?"

"Not yet. But her mom's pregnant, so she will." A masculine smile crawled across his lips. "I guess the old guy is pretty potent."

Susan rolled her eyes. "Spoken like a true man."

The smile remained. "What can I say? He handed out cigars when he found out. He seemed proud."

And Cathy appeared to have a nice family, but appearances could be deceiving. "Why do you think she's so rebellious? Does she seem jealous that her parents are having another baby? Or embarrassed by it?"

"I don't know. But I think she prefers to interact with animals more than people. She pretends that Chocolate annoys her, but I've seen her slipping him treats. And she hangs around the barn before school, bringing carrots to the horses."

"Maybe that's the way I can reach her." She snared his gaze. "Maybe we both can."

"That kid isn't interested in being reached. She's a loner."

"Who prefers animals to people. Like you did when you were young."

"Fine." He softened his voice. "Next time you see her, you can ask her if she wants to go on a ride along."

"With you?" Her heart made a grateful little leap toward his. "On your rounds?"

"Yes, but you have to come, too."

She agreed, and they looked at each other from across the table. Friends, she thought. And saviors of lost teenage souls.

If not Cathy's, then at least their own.

Chapter 5

Ethan entered the barn and walked the first row of stalls. Dinner had ended on a tender note last night, and he'd gone to bed thinking about Susan, anxious to see her again.

So here he was, the following morning, scouting the ranch for her, hoping his instincts paid off.

And they did. Just a few minutes later when he saw her standing at Serene's stall.

Rather than make his presence known, he stopped and watched her. She fed the mare an apple wedge, and the horse gobbled it up. After Serene nudged her for another bite, Susan laughed and obliged the determined Appaloosa.

"Are you spoiling my horse?" he finally said.

Susan spun around, and he smiled at her. For a moment, time seemed to stand still. She smiled at him, too. Serene chomped noisily in the background, but it didn't matter. A connection had already been made.

"Did you bring Chocolate with you?" he asked, wondering why the dog wasn't driving them nuts.

"He's still asleep in my bed."

Lucky mutt, Ethan thought. He suspected her bed was warm and silky, overflowing with pillows and scented with a hint of lemon.

"Are you working today?" she asked.

"Not until later." He kept his gaze riveted to hers. "I came here looking for you because I knew you'd come here looking for Cathy. Did you find her?"

"No. I checked behind the outbuildings first, but there was no sign of her."

"I guess she picked a new spot to sneak a smoke."

"So it seems." She broke eye contact, looking around. "Does she come to the barn every morning or is this a long shot?"

"I don't know. I'm not here every day. But I've seen her quite a few times, dressed for school, with her backpack and all that."

"Making friends with the horses?"

"Yep." He moved closer. "Like you just did with Serene."

She moved closer, too, meeting him halfway. "I couldn't come here empty-handed."

"Me, neither. I have a thermos of coffee in the truck and some store-bought muffins. Do you want to join me for breakfast?"

She tucked her hair behind her ears, and he noticed a set of diamonds studs. They looked good on her, even with a simple button-down blouse and cowgirl-cut jeans.

"I'd love to have breakfast with you," she said. "But do you realize that all we ever do when we're together is eat?"

"Really? Hmm." He stuffed his hands in his pockets. "Maybe we just need to keep our mouths busy."

She sucked her bottom lip between her teeth, and he knew he'd struck a chord. She wanted to kiss him as badly as he wanted to kiss her. But they kept eating instead.

"What kind of muffins?" she asked.

"Blueberry," he told her. Now she was moistening her lips, making a blast of arousal swirl in his gut.

She untucked her hair, letting it fall against her cheeks once again. "Did you add cream and sugar to the coffee?"

"No, but I brought those little packets." He

made a goofy face, trying to temper the heat that was headed straight for his groin. "I always nab them from fast-food joints."

She laughed a little. "I guess it's a bachelor thing."

"Or a cheap thing. I should probably break down and buy them." He removed his hands from his pockets, concerned about calling attention to his zipper. "Are you ready to sample my coffee?"

"Is it strong?"

"Always."

"Then I'm ready."

They walked outside together. Ethan barely noticed the scent of hay and horses. For him, it was as familiar as his own sweat at the end of a hard-earned day.

He got the thermos and muffins out of his truck, setting up their breakfast on the bed of his vehicle.

Seated next to Susan, he handed her a disposable cup, then poured her coffee and watched it steam in the morning air.

She doctored her drink, making it sweet and light, stirring it with a plastic spoon he'd provided. He drank his black, using the thermos cup.

She gave him an odd look. "Why do you take these packets if you don't use them?"

"For company. For people who come to visit. Or for times like this."

She removed a muffin from the package and picked at the blueberries, nibbling like a bird. "I'm a morning person. I like to get up early and embrace the day."

"Me, too." As crumbs dropped onto her lap, Ethan realized that he'd forgotten about napkins. But it didn't matter. She seemed comfortable by his side, making him curious to know more about her. "Tell me about your job. Do you share your office with other psychologists?"

She answered easily, quickly. "I don't have a private practice. I run a national youth crisis hotline. We guide troubled teens, getting them the help they need."

Silent, he rubbed his hand across his jaw. It made perfect sense. A national hotline fit her: the girl she used to be and the woman she'd become. Yet he'd envisioned her in a high-rise building, treating rich kids whose parents were footing the bill.

"It's difficult to take time off," she said. "But my assistant is filling in for me. There's always so much to do, almost more than any of us—the employees and the volunteers—can handle."

"What sort of issues do you cover?"

"Everything. Emotional, spiritual and social problems. Anything a teenager might face today. Sometimes it's easier for them to call a hotline and talk to a stranger than approach someone they know. And the hotline is available twenty-four hours a day." The noise from ranch hands repairing a fence made hollow sounds, echoing in the distance. "I need to make a difference, to devote my life to something that offers kids a choice."

He sipped his coffee, letting the hot beverage settle in his bones. "What was wrong when you were young, Susan? What happened between you and your dad?"

She looked up, her eyes suddenly more hazel than green, something that happened when she turned sad. He used to study her, storing all of her gestures, habits and physical traits in his mind. The way she did with him, he supposed. They were both guilty of dissecting each other.

"My dad was a respected banker in our community," she said. "But he was also a functioning alcoholic."

"And abusive?"

She nodded. "Nothing any of us ever did was right. Vincent tried to protect us, but it didn't help."

Ethan waited for her to continue. He knew Vincent was her oldest brother, a man who'd become a security specialist.

"I was primed for a rebellion," she said. "To prove that I could fight fire with fire."

And destroy her own innocence, he thought. A drinker, a smoker, a girl who'd tried to make boys like her by giving them sexual favors, by laying her young soul on the line.

She set her half-eaten muffin on top of the wrapper. "My dad and I had a horrible fight one night. I came home late, drunk as a lipstick-smeared skunk, and he blew a gasket. The ironic part is that he was wasted, too. Bleary-eyed from all those proper martinis. But he didn't see it that way. He always made excuses for himself." She reached for her coffee and held the cup against her chest. "He kicked me out, told me to go live on the streets. But my mother, passive as she was, reminded him that I was too young to be on my own. So Dad decided to pawn me off on the first relative who was willing to take me."

"Ryan," Ethan said, tempted to touch her, to absorb the texture of her skin.

She nodded, her breathing soft and gentle, as light as the breeze that whispered in the wind. "He was my salvation. I spent almost a year defying him, going around this ranch, acting tough and getting into trouble. But toward the end, I realized how much he and his family cared about me." She smiled at the memory. "Ryan treated me like one of his own children. The way a child should be treated. He held me accountable when I broke the rules, but he praised me when I did something right. He was proud of my academic achievements. He said kind things to me. He encouraged me to apply to prestigious colleges, to show the world what I was made of."

Inner strength, Ethan thought. And a reckless nature she'd learned to tame. "How is the rest of your family doing?" he asked, wondering about her siblings. He'd never met them, not officially, but he knew who they were.

"Vincent got married a couple months ago," she said. "He's on an extended honeymoon, but it's mainly to keep his wife out of danger. She witnessed a murder and the killer is still at large." She paused, frowned. "It's Jason Jamison, the man who threatened Ryan. You know about him, don't you?"

"Yes. Ryan told me about him. He's the reason security is so tight around here." And now he understood why Ryan hadn't hired Vincent's company to do the job. Vincent was out of town.

Susan resumed their conversation. "My brother Daniel is doing fine. He's married, too. His wife's name is Alisha. They ran off to Vegas last weekend without telling anyone." She managed a lighthearted laugh. "I never thought that would happen to him. Falling in love so deeply."

Ethan didn't know if he should envy or pity the guy. "And your sister?"

"Kyra?" She made a thoughtful expression. "She's just Kyra. Tall, stylish and distrustful of men."

"So are you," he said.

"Distrustful of men?"

"No." He shot her a boyish grin. "Stylish. But she's got you beat in the tall department."

"Don't I know it?" She jammed her elbow into him. "But don't act superior. You like petite blondes."

"That I do." He balanced his coffee as it sloshed in his cup. He'd patterned every blonde he'd ever dated after her. Not consciously, but he'd done it.

A Freudian crime, he mused, recalling how she'd teased him about it last night.

When silence lapsed between them, they sat quietly, watching the ranch hands do their jobs. Ethan finished his muffin, but Susan still picked at hers like a sparrow.

"I never made peace with him," she said. "But at the time I didn't want to. So, in the end, there was nothing. No closure."

He knew she was taking about her father. "I heard your parents died in a single-vehicle accident."

"Seven years ago. Dad was driving." She turned to look at him. "We never knew if he'd been drinking. We never found out."

He put his arm around her, holding her close, giving her the comfort she needed. She closed her eyes and rested her head on his shoulder.

He closed his eyes, too. He knew what it was

like to cut someone out of his heart, to not make peace with that person. But he wasn't going to offer information about his mom and what she'd done to his dad, a man who was kind and loyal, unlike the bastard who'd sired Susan.

Some things, Ethan thought, were better left unsaid.

After spending the morning with Ethan, after being wrapped in his arms, Susan entered the house and stood in the foyer, feeling warm and protected. But the feeling didn't last long.

Deep, serious voices caught her attention, bringing her back to reality. Ryan and another man were discussing Jason Jamison. She couldn't see them, but she could hear them, just a heartbeat away, in the great room. Was Lily there, too, sitting quietly, anxiety churning inside her?

As Susan moved toward the voices, her boots sounded on the tiled floor, signaling her presence. Everyone turned to look at her. Ryan, Lily and the other man.

Was he the head of the security team?

He stood next to Ryan, and she realized that whoever he was, he was preparing to leave. That their discussion was over, at least for now.

He was tall, with short dark hair and a strong, solid build. His clothes were as dark as his hair and the expression on his face.

"Susan," Ryan spoke first. "This is Special Agent Jamison. Emmett," he added, using the other man's first name, letting her know she didn't have to stand on formality.

So this was Jason's brother? The FBI agent who'd vowed to track him down?

She extended her hand. "Nice to meet you. I'm Ryan and Lily's cousin. I don't live here. I'm visiting from California."

"I know who you are. I'm aware of everyone on the ranch."

Of course, she thought. That was part of his job.

Emmett's manner, she noticed, was professional yet brusque. Even his handshake was quick and to the point. But that didn't mean he wasn't aware of his surroundings. His eyes, as green as her own, cut through her like a blade. When she took a step back, his gaze didn't leave her face, not until he turned away to address Ryan.

"I'll be in touch," he told him.

"I appreciate it." Ryan looked old and tired next to the sharp-eyed man. But he'd probably had a trying day, fighting the tumor that swelled his brain. His symptoms were getting worse.

Emmett nodded at Lily, saying goodbye to her, a salutation the woman returned. Behind her, the doors that led to the inner courtyard were open, creating a picturesque backdrop, flowers blooming at every turn. The setting didn't fit Emmett

Jamison. It seemed too bright, too cheerful for his hard-edged demeanor.

The special agent departed, not through the inner courtyard, but through the front door, where another courtyard and a wrought-iron gate prevailed. Ryan disappeared with him, leaving the women by themselves.

"Emmett isn't what I expected," Susan said.

"Me, neither." Lily paused, her eyebrows knit. "But he must be a good man. Ryan seems to like him, to sense his honor."

Susan nodded. Her cousin was a strong judge of character, at least most of the time. He'd trusted Jason in the beginning. "Any word on Jason's whereabouts?"

"Not yet, but Emmett is doing what he can to find him."

"I'm sure he is." But in spite of Ryan's confidence in the FBI agent, Susan could tell that Lily was still fighting her fears. Emmett was only human. As were the members of the security team patrolling the ranch. Jason had foiled police and prison guards, making him a dangerously clever man. A criminal who was giving Lily chills.

The older woman rubbed her arms, then glanced at the coffee service that sat on a hand-carved table. "Would you like a cup?" she asked Susan.

"No, thanks. I had coffee with Ethan this morning."

That made Lily smile. "I'm glad you rediscovered him."

She thought about the way he'd held her. "Me, too."

Just then Ryan entered the room, looking even more tired than before. Feeble, uncoordinated. But proud, so incredibly proud. He struggled to control his impaired speech. "If you ladies don't mind, I'm going to lie down for a while."

Lily walked over to her husband. "Of course we don't mind."

Susan should have glanced away, giving the older couple a stolen moment of privacy, but she watched them, her heart thumping in her chest. Ryan touched his wife's cheek, and she covered his unsteady hand with hers. A man and a woman who'd been in love since they were teenagers, who'd rediscovered each other years later.

Like Susan and Ethan.

No, she told herself. She wasn't in love with Ethan, and he wasn't in love with her. It wasn't the same.

When Ryan departed, Lily stood in the middle of the room, looking far too alone. She hugged herself, rumpling a cotton blouse. A pleated skirt flowed to her ankles and a pair of nonfringed moccasins made a simple, soft-spoken statement.

Susan approached her, taking her hand, holding it gently. When Lily was young, she didn't think she deserved Ryan. A poor Indian girl and a rich Texas heir. They'd come a long way, Susan thought.

"Don't start missing him," she told Lily. "Not now, not while he's still part of our lives."

"I'm trying to be strong."

"You are strong." Susan turned to face her, still holding her hand, still lending support. "You're everything he needs."

Lily smiled through watery eyes, stifling her tears, refusing to cry. "Let's go outside. We can look through the photo albums I was working on before Emmett showed up."

Susan followed Lily into the courtyard, where a glass table held a stack of leather-bound albums. Loose photos, some with aged and yellowed edges, were secured in a plastic container, the lid held tight. "Did you show Emmett pictures of our family?"

"Goodness, no." Lily pulled out a chair. "He doesn't seem interested in our personal affairs. That man is strictly business."

"It's strange, though, knowing he's related to the Fortunes. Of course that's what started this mess. His brother wanting a piece of the pie."

"Jason wanted the whole pie." Lily sat down,

inviting Susan to do the same. "Emmett is nothing like him."

A moment later they paged through the first album. Lily treated each photograph with reverence, even those that presented images of Ryan's first wife.

Ryan's second wife was another matter. There were no pictures of her, at least not in Lily's care. But the second Mrs. Fortune, who'd met with a violent demise, had used Ryan for his money, and Lily, of all people, had been accused of murdering her.

But that seemed like a lifetime ago, Susan thought. A storm Ryan and Lily had weathered.

"I want to show you something." Lily reached for another album and opened it to the last page.

Susan gazed at the picture of a young boy with blond hair and blues eyes. He smiled for the camera, yet somehow he seemed lost.

"Who is he?" she asked.

"Ricky Faraday." Lily touched the picture, almost as though she meant to smooth his hair, to brush a lock that fell onto his forehead. "He's ten years old, and he's Cameron Fortune's son."

Susan took a closer look at the picture. "Cameron? Ryan's brother?"

"Ricky was born after Cameron died, but Ryan kept it a secret. His mother, Linda Faraday, was in the car with Cameron when he crashed it. But she didn't die. She went into a temporary coma, then a semi-conscious state later."

"While she was pregnant with Ricky?"

Lily nodded. "She recovered, but it's been a long, hard road. At first she was in a nursing home, and now she's in a rehabilitation facility. She's able to visit Ricky, and he visits her, but their relationship is strained. They barely know each other."

"Where does Ricky live?" Susan asked. "Who takes care of him?"

"Ryan found a foster home for Ricky a long time ago, with an elderly couple who treat him like a grandson." She glanced up. "I've gotten close to Linda and Ricky, too. I've had the opportunity to spend some time with them. But it breaks my heart to see them so distant from each other."

Susan touched the boy's picture. "Time is supposed to heal all wounds."

"I hope so," Lily whispered. "But you can't tell anyone about this. I only told you because you're a psychologist. And because—"

"You needed to talk about it?"

"Yes."

Susan assured her that she wouldn't repeat any of it. That she would keep the secret.

"What does Linda look like?" she asked, wondering about the woman who'd given birth to Cameron's son.

"She's stunning," came the instant reply. "Long blond hair, striking features. But she's fragile, too. Someone a man, a good man," Lily added with a slight pause, "would want to protect."

Emmett checked into the Corner Inn and walked across the street to what he considered a nameless, faceless diner. He entered the greasy-spoon establishment and looked around. He'd been in places like this all over the map. Red vinyl booths and a counter near the cash register that displayed day-old pies in clear, plastic cases.

He took a seat at the counter, and a down-home waitress handed him a menu and offered him coffee, which he accepted with a none-too-friendly nod. Emmett wasn't in the mood for small-town chatter.

Out of the corner of his eye, he caught sight of a fair-haired boy eating lunch with his family. But it was the family that gave him pause. An older couple, probably the kid's grandparents, sat on either side of him, happily sandwiching the boy. The youngster didn't seem to mind. If anything, he appeared comfortable with the gray-haired duo. It was the blonde seated across from him who made the child frown.

A woman, Emmett noticed. His mother? His older sister? Emmett couldn't tell. All he could see was the back of her head and a long, flowing mane of golden hair.

Turning away, Emmett scanned his menu. He had enough childhood memories locked away in his own troubled mind. He didn't need to concern himself with someone else's family.

Nothing could be as bad as claiming a killer, as having a man like Jason for a brother.

The waitress returned, and he ordered a burger and fries. The kid at the corner booth had been eating the same meal. Emmett cursed his curiosity and took a quick glance in that direction. The older couple seemed a bit too chipper, as if they were trying to make everything all right. But the boy's expression faltered every time he looked across the table at the blonde.

Who was she? Emmett wondered. And why did she make an innocent child struggle with his emotions?

She had pretty hair, that much Emmett could attest to. Which was a stupid, superficial thought, he told himself. An observance that didn't deserve merit.

By the time his food arrived, Emmett filled his empty belly and ignored the other patrons in the restaurant, including the boy and the blonde.

They didn't factor into his life. Or the reason

he'd come to Red Rock. Catching a killer was his only agenda.

And he wouldn't rest until it was done.

Chapter 6

Susan couldn't sleep. She squinted at the digital clock beside her bed and wondered if Ethan was still awake. Should she take a chance and call?

She couldn't explain her restlessness, the feeling that something was wrong. Then again, a lot of things were wrong. Ryan was dying, and Lily was trying to hold on to every ounce of strength she had.

As for herself, she wanted to make everything better for both of them, to erase the pain in their lives.

But she couldn't. Not completely.

Wavering with temptation, she picked up the

portable phone from its cradle and held the device in her hand.

Call him, her heart said.

And say what? her mind asked.

She glanced at the clock again, and Chocolate stirred beside her, too sleepy to open his eyes.

Having Ethan's dog close by should be enough. But it wasn't. She wanted to hear Ethan's voice. She wanted him to soothe her discontented soul.

The phone grew warm in her hand, and she loosened her grip, trying to remember the number she'd written in her day planner.

Finally, she gave up and opened the top drawer for her little black book.

The connotation made her smile, then frown, then sigh. Seventeen years ago, her number had been scribbled in a lot of little black books. And on a few bathroom walls, too.

She dialed the digits that would connect her to Ethan, listening to each tone beep in her ear. When his phone started to ring, her nerves danced on the hot-tin roof of her heart.

"Hello," he answered, but he didn't sound groggy. If anything, he sounded overly awake.

She wondered if he was having trouble sleeping, too. "It's me."

"Susan? Is everything all right?"

"I'm just a little restless." She paused and snuggled into bed, nudging Chocolate, who didn't budge an inch. "I needed to hear a friendly voice."

"Then I'm all yours."

All six gorgeous feet of him, she thought. "What were you doing before I called?"

"Watching cable TV, but there's nothing on."

"What channel?" she asked, expecting him to say Animal Planet. Every time she watched it, she thought of him.

"Playboy," he said.

She blinked, kicked out her legs and caught her toes on the blanket. "What?"

"The Playboy Channel. That's what I was watching."

He subscribed to that? "I thought you said nothing was on?"

"It was boring. It seemed like nothing."

"Liar," she challenged, and made him laugh.

"Okay, so it was sexy. But talking to you is better."

Oh, he was good, she thought. Practiced in the art of seduction. Or was it deception? At this point she couldn't be sure. "Did you turn it off?"

"No." He lowered his voice. "I just turned down the sound."

"So you can still see it?"

"Uh-huh."

She imagined him angling his head, gazing at naked women on the screen. Or maybe he was viewing naked couples. Soft porn or whatever the Playboy Channel promoted.

"Tell me what your room looks like," he said.

When her mouth went dry, she moistened her lips. "Which room? The one in San Francisco or the one I'm staying in here?"

"Where you're at now. I want to picture the bed. I want to imagine you in it."

Uh-oh. She should have known better than to call a man after midnight. Especially a hunky Texan who admitted that he wanted to sleep with her.

"What color are the sheets?" he pressed.

"White."

"And the blanket?"

"Mauve."

"What's that? Pink?"

"Yes, but it's sort of an icy pink. Like nail polish or lipstick."

"Mmm." He made a moaning sound. "So it's a girlie room?"

"It's the same one I had when I lived here. It was always sort of girlie. A female guest room, I guess." She pictured him in the hunting cabin, stretched out on the sofa bed, talking to her and watching naughty TV. A hot-blooded male in a primal environment.

"I wish you were here," he said. "Or I was there."

"Me, too," she admitted, knowing they were playing a dangerous game. The next time they saw each other, this conversation would float between them like a dream. "But this is crazy. We're crazy."

His voice turned raw. "I know."

Susan wondered if he was aroused, hard and thick against his jeans or whatever he was wearing.

She wasn't about to ask. "Maybe we should hang up."

"I don't want to. Do you?"

"No." She couldn't bear to lose him, to sever the tie. Not yet. "Why don't we change the subject? Think of something safe to say."

"Like what?"

She racked her brain, then laid eyes on Chocolate. "Your dog snores. And he sleeps with his butt in the air."

Ethan went silent, then chuckled under his breath. A moment later a rustling sound came from his end of the line, as if he were moving, reaching for the remote to turn off the TV. "I forgot that damn mutt was there."

She smiled, grateful that she'd just blown his fantasy. And better yet, abolished the Playboy instigator. "Do you want to talk to him?"

"Funny girl. Do you want to talk to the dogs that are sleeping with me?"

A laugh bubbled from her throat. "I guess that makes us even." He'd just blown her fantasy, too. "Maybe they should talk to each other."

"Maybe." He took a deep breath and released it into the receiver. "Are you feeling better?"

She nodded, then realized he couldn't see her. "Yes. I'm not so restless anymore. I think I'll be able to sleep tonight."

"Good. I like being your friend, Susan."

Her heart nearly squeezed its way through the phone. "That means a lot to me, Ethan."

"Then close your eyes, and I'll stay here until you fall asleep."

"Okay," she whispered, knowing it was the perfect way to spend the night with him, to rest in his phantom arms.

Ryan remained as still as a corpse, afraid he would disturb Lily. He'd been awake for hours, staring at the ceiling, at make-believe patterns on the walls.

He turned to look at his wife. Like a bat in an underground cave, he could see her in the dark because his eyes had adjusted to the absence of light.

She looked so pretty, with her hair fanned across a pillow and her nightgown clinging to her body like a 3:00 a.m. rain.

Ryan didn't want to leave her. He didn't want to die.

When his breath clogged his lungs, he sat up, his body stiff from the rigid motion, from remaining still for so long. He flexed his legs, trying to regain use of his limbs.

Having a tumor was a bitch.

Desperate for some air, he reached for the clothes he'd deliberately left on a chair and grabbed his boots, tiptoeing, a bit sideways, to the sitting area and heading for the door.

Lily sighed in her sleep, and he hoped that she was dreaming. A good dream. Something heavenly.

He got dressed in the hall, then took care of his pajamas. As quietly as possible, he rumpled them into a ball and tossed them back into the room, where they landed in the sitting area like the ghosts that haunted Topper. Ryan smiled to himself, remembering those screwball comedies. Cary Grant classics, filmed even before he was born.

Being a ghost wouldn't be so bad, he decided. Not if life imitated art. But he knew it didn't. He wouldn't return from the dead to star in a madcap movie.

Once he was gone, it was over. Finished. He would never see Lily again.

With his heart twisting in his chest, he picked up the phone in the kitchen and called the main security line, letting them know he was going for a walk.

The officer didn't question his motives, but this wasn't the first time he'd strolled the grounds at this hour. Ryan was becoming a regular night owl.

But hey, rich folks were known for being eccentric.

At least Lily never found out. He always returned before she awakened, before she could worry about her husband's insomnia.

After he ended the call, he left through the back door and went outside, anxious to absorb the land that had become his legacy.

The Double Crown Ranch.

He spotted a security vehicle that was parked beside the perimeter of the backyard and waved to the guard who was manning it. He received a wave in return, realizing all of the officers on duty had been informed through their communication system that the old man was playing vampire again.

A rancher. A humanitarian. A ghoul of the night.

It struck Ryan as funny. But it struck him as sad, too.

He wondered if his father would be waiting for him in the afterlife, if Kingston Fortune would lead him into the white light.

And what about Cameron, his older brother?

The ultracharming, drinking, gambling party boy who'd left a comatose woman and an unborn child behind? Ryan wasn't sure if he wanted to see Cameron again, even if Linda and Ricky had survived the pain Cam had put them through.

Ryan had done right by Linda and her son, but he was still worried about them, wishing he could find a young, noble man to look after them when he was gone.

But that was what he wanted for all of the women in his family. Gallant knights, dragon slayers who loved them.

The way he loved Lily.

Ryan kept walking, away from the prying eyes of the security guard and into the night. He needed to be alone, to think, to reminisce.

He didn't want his dragon slayer days to be over, even if his legs were getting weak, even if the darkness threatened to swallow him.

And then it did. Within the blink of an eye, someone grabbed him from behind, covering his mouth and making it impossible to breathe.

"Susan?" Ethan said her name, whispering into the phone. Had she fallen asleep? Drifted into a sensuous slumber?

She didn't respond, but he didn't have the strength to hang up on her.

Beautiful Susan. The girl of his boyhood dreams.

He took the phone into the kitchen and opened the refrigerator, where the light poured over the cracker-box room like a message from God.

He frowned and grabbed a beer, hoping the Creator didn't mind. One of his mixed-breed mutts trailed after him, then barked, asking to go outside.

Still cradling the phone, he walked to the front door and opened it, where the dog took off, anxious to pee.

Ethan looked into the darkness. The world was still, the night waxed by a three-quarter moon. He couldn't see the main house where Susan was. The hunting cabin was miles away.

He pulled on the beer and imagined holding her, losing himself in her luxurious scent. It was crazy to get so wrapped up in a woman, to feel this way, but he couldn't help it.

Restless, he sat on his front porch and counted the stars. "There's thirteen," he said into the phone, to the girl who slept on the other line.

Was that unlucky?

Did that mean that something was wrong?

Shrugging away the superstition, he told himself to relax. Susan was safe. She was right there, next to him, connected through telephone wires.

If he listened hard enough, he could hear her

soft, feminine breathing. Nothing was wrong, he insisted. No late-night mishaps. No prowlers. No bad guys. No witches soaring across the moon.

Nothing but the sleep that eluded him.

Emmett flipped on the light and jerked out of bed. He looked around his motel room, but no one was there. Only the nightmares that plagued him, like demons seeping into his pores, making him sweat.

He walked over to the sliding-glass door and opened it, stepping onto the balcony, breathing in the night air.

A breeze caressed his face and he glanced across the street at the diner. It was closed, the security lights dim and morguelike.

Death in a small town.

He ran his hand through his hair and cursed his brother. He could feel Jason. Here. There. Everywhere.

A killer, he thought. Just waiting to strike.

Was that instinct or paranoia? he asked himself.

Emmett hadn't been on a hunt in a very long time. And he'd never hunted his own. Was he too damn close to the situation? Was he chasing shadows? Or was this the real deal?

He returned to the motel room and glanced at the bedside clock. Four-fifteen in the morning was a hell of a time to have doubts. But even so, he couldn't go back to sleep, not on his first night in Texas.

Because Emmett suspected that Jason knew right where he was.

Lily awakened in the dark and reached for Ryan, but his spot beside her was empty. Concerned, she turned on the lamp and battled with an ominous feeling.

But when didn't she?

Blowing out the breath in her lungs, she climbed out of bed and checked the adjoining bathroom, but Ryan wasn't there. As she entered the sitting area, she discovered his pajamas strewn across the floor.

Deciding to search the rest of the house, Lily walked down the hall and saw that Susan's light was on. Was everyone awake at this hour? Curious, she peeked into the young woman's room. Susan was asleep with the phone pressed to her ear. Unusual as it was, the scenario gave Lily comfort. She suspected that Ethan was on the other end, keeping Susan company while she drifted in and out of girlish dreams.

Lily continued looking for Ryan, but she couldn't find him anywhere. Not even in the garage, where men often disappeared. And since none of their vehicles were missing, he hadn't left the ranch. Not unless someone drove him to his desired destination. But who? And where?

Confused, she picked up the phone in the kitchen, a different line from the one in Susan's room, and dialed security, asking if they'd seen her husband.

And much to her surprise, the guard on phone duty explained that Ryan went for a walk in the backyard, something he'd done several times this week.

"He's headed back to the house," the man said. "We've been keeping an eye on him. From afar," he added. "We never let him get out of sight for too long, but Mr. Fortune doesn't like us to disturb him at night."

"I see."

"Yes, ma'am. Will there be anything else?"

"No. Thank you." She ended the call and shook her head, wondering what had possessed Ryan to traipse around in the dark.

His tumor, she thought. And the odd behavior it sometimes caused. Her husband wasn't himself.

With a sigh, she put a pan of milk on the stove, needing to drink something warm, something comforting. When Ryan returned, she would offer to go on his next walk with him, to share his late-night jaunts.

What else could she do? Reprimand a dying man?

After the milk was done, she poured it into a cup and carried it into the dining room.

Seated at the table, she sipped slowly, deliberately, waiting for Ryan. The back door opened and his footsteps soundly softly. Too softly, she thought. He was trying to sneak back into the house.

"I'm in here," she called out, letting him know she was awake. He would panic if he didn't find her in bed.

Silence. More footsteps. Then a familiar voice. A voice from hell.

"Lily, my love."

She spun around and knocked over her milk.

Jason lunged at her, covering her mouth with a cloth. There was no time to scream. She smelled the chemical beneath her nose, felt its dizzying effect instantly.

Her brain floated outside of her body, trying to make sense of what was happening, of the confusion, the fear, the man whispering in her ear.

"I was coming to your bedroom, sweet Lily. Coming to take you with me. But here you are."

"Ry...an..." She said her husband's name, but it was garbled, like a record on a turntable, moving forward, backward, spinning at the wrong speed.

"Don't worry about Ryan. I drugged him, too. Then I took his place. Your rent-a-cops thought I was him." He tied a gag around her mouth and secured her hands behind her back. As she tried to pull away, a maniacal smile spread across his face, melting his features like wax. "I even waved to the security guards, like he does. And I'm wearing his shirt. They didn't know the difference."

Jason pushed her onto the floor, where she flopped like a rag doll. She looked up at him, but his face kept getting more and more distorted.

He spoke quietly, even though Susan was sleeping in a different wing of the house. "Now all I have to do is call those imbeciles and tell them that my wife and I are going for a drive and we don't want to be disturbed."

No, she thought. No. Most women who were abducted never came home. Getting into a madman's car was the kiss of death.

She looked for an escape, but she could barely move, the drugged sensation getting worse.

As Lily's thoughts spun in a confusing circle, Jason walked away and made the call, pretending to be Ryan.

"I pressed redial." He came back, leering at her. "Brilliant, isn't it? I didn't even need the number."

He went down the hall and suddenly she feared he was going to kidnap Susan, too. But he didn't. He returned with Lily's pocketbook, then dug through it, stealing her cash and retrieving her keys.

"We'll take your car. That shiny new truck of

yours." When he lifted her up, she stumbled, fighting a wave of nausea, the bile suppressed in the back of her throat.

He pulled her into the garage and shoved her into the front seat, where she sagged against the window, knowing she was only seconds away from losing consciousness.

From disappearing off the face of the earth.

Chapter 7

The FBI was everywhere, Susan thought. All over the ranch, questioning everyone on the premises. In the main house, where she and Ryan were, they'd set up equipment, preparing to trace incoming calls.

Another team of agents was searching for Lily, but they hadn't found her.

Susan glanced at Ryan. At daybreak, a security guard had come across him, unconscious and hidden behind some shrubs. Of course by the time all hell broke loose, Lily had been missing for several hours.

Ryan had refused to remain at the hospital,

where he'd been examined earlier. So here he was, seated beside Susan on a leather couch in the great room, still a little sluggish from the chemical Jason had pressed against his nose and mouth.

Her cousin knew it was Jason who'd drugged him. The other man had whispered in his ear, bragging about himself, while Ryan had struggled to fight back, a battle he hadn't been able to win.

He turned to look at Susan, and a myriad of emotions crossed his face. Pain, guilt, anger. She searched his gaze, but suddenly he seemed lifeless, empty inside.

He was lost without Lily.

Susan was lost, too, but she couldn't break down. Ryan needed her. Even so, horrible images kept sluicing through her mind. She had no idea what Jason would do to Lily; what he might have done to her already.

Chocolate came toward her, then settled down at her feet. He seemed confused by all the people. Earlier he'd roamed from room to room, as though he were looking for Lily, trying to find her in the midst of the chaos he couldn't begin to understand.

Susan shifted her gaze to the dining room, where Emmett Jamison was grilling the security guards who'd been on duty last night.

The special agent had been questioning them

for what seemed like hours, but he continued his relentless pursuit. Was he suspicious of them? Did he think they were involved in the abduction? That they'd aided Jason? Or was he simply trying to piece together the puzzle, to gather every clue, to reenact the scenario in his mind?

Susan had no idea if Emmett was officially assigned to the case or if he was there on his own. The house was filled with FBI investigators, as well as members of a crisis negotiation team.

"I have to look for her," Ryan said suddenly.

He shot up, wobbling like a drunken sailor, constricting the air in Susan's lungs. She remained close, ready to catch him if he fell. Chocolate lifted his head, watching Ryan through puppy-dog eyes.

"Lily would want you to stay home," she told him. "To wait for her."

"But I can't stand it. I can't sit around and do nothing." He held on to the side of the couch. "This is my fault. I'm the one who abandoned her."

"No." Susan shook her head. "You didn't do this. Jason did. This is his fault."

"I shouldn't have gone for that damn walk." His entire body vibrated. "I shouldn't have left her alone."

"She wasn't alone. I was in the house, sleeping in another wing." She paused, caught his gaze, felt her heart beat frantically in her chest. "Do you think it's my fault, too?"

His voice all but cracked. "No, of course not."

"Then don't blame yourself, either." She implored him with strength, with gentleness, with the guilt that was tugging at her own conscience.

Unable to remain standing, he slumped back down. He hadn't cried yet, but Susan knew he would. When he was by himself, when no one could see him.

Emmett stopped grilling the security guards, and a moment of silence ensued. He grabbed a dining-room chair and carried it into the great room, scooting it close to the couch. Chocolate gave him a curious look.

"We're doing our best to find your wife," the agent said, speaking softly to Ryan. "We have a team of agents searching for her."

"I know."

"Did Jason say anything to you that might help us find her? Anything to indicate where he might take her?"

"No. Nothing. Only that he was making good on his threat."

"To harm someone in your family?"

Ryan's voice quavered. "Yes."

Emmett didn't react, at least not outwardly. But Susan suspected that his stomach was tied up in knots. His brother, his own flesh and blood, had just gotten away with another crime.

"As far as I can tell," he said, addressing her and Ryan, "Jason acted alone. He's probably been casing the ranch, waiting for an opportunity to strike." He looked at Ryan. "He must have known that you go for walks at night. He must have seen you on other occasions."

Before Ryan could start blaming himself again, Susan reached for his hand, holding on to him, linking their fingers. "Jason has been on the property before?" she asked Emmett. "While the security team was patrolling the grounds?"

"Most likely, ma'am. This is a big ranch, with plenty of places for someone to slip through the cracks. We're still investigating the situation, but we think he's been camping in the hills, hiking his way down to the ranch and hiding out in the line shack when no one's around."

"It doesn't matter." Ryan squeezed Susan's hand. "If I would have stayed with Lily, if I hadn't given Jason the opportunity to impersonate me, none of this would have happened."

"You had no way of knowing what Jason was going to do." Susan tried to keep her cousin calm. But his emotions teetered on the edge, up and down, side to side, like a jackknifed seesaw.

When he gazed at her, she struggled not to cry. He was looking at her as if she were a teenager, the young girl who'd come to live with him all those years ago.

"He could have taken you, too," Ryan said.

"But he didn't," she responded.

"You need someone to protect you."

"I'm going to be fine."

"A woman needs a man in her life. Someone who cares, someone who won't leave her side."

Susan's heart sank to the pit of her stomach. Ryan wouldn't stop blaming himself. "Wherever Lily is, she knows that you love her."

"Yes, but it's not the same as protecting her." Still holding Susan's hand, he turned to Emmett, his question laced with trepidation, with fear of the unknown. "What do you think Jason's next move is going to be?"

The agent came forward in his chair. "I think he's going to demand a ransom. But I'm not allowed to advise you."

"I don't need advice, not about this." Ryan steeled his emotions. "I'll pay him whatever he wants. Anything to get Lily back."

"And that's what he'll be relying on." A muscle in Emmett's jaw twitched. "Ransom-oriented abductions are rare. Most criminals know it's next to impossible to succeed, but I think Jason will be willing to take that risk."

"He's cocky," Susan said.

"And delusional." Emmett's same muscle

twitched, like a bullet beneath his skin. "We're not dealing with a rational man. Jason is hell-bent on enacting his revenge."

A moment later he fell silent. Cautious about saying too much, Susan thought, about making things more difficult for Ryan. He wouldn't dare comment on the pain his brother could inflict, on what Jason might do to Lily. But she was certain that it had crossed his mind, too many times to count.

She wanted to cry for Ryan. And God help them, for Lily, the lost and beautiful lady who'd been fearful all along.

The love of Ryan's life. The heartbeat of his world.

She said a silent prayer and caught the FBI agent watching her, his eyes filled with intensity, with the rage he'd yet to express.

If push came to shove, he would kill his brother, hold a gun to his chest and make him accountable for his sins. That much Susan could tell.

"Jason did this to all of us," she said, meeting his gaze.

"Yes, he did. And I doubt he's going to contact us right away. He'll probably make us wait. For as long as it takes," he added, glancing at Ryan, telling him, without words, to remain strong.

To not give up hope.

* * *

Evening came with a hush, with no news of Lily. Patrick Fortune, Susan's seventy-year-old uncle, arrived at the ranch to stay with Ryan. Patrick had recently retired as the president of Fortune-Rockwell banking, but he still had access to the company. Susan suspected that he was going to help Ryan gather the ransom when—or if—a ransom was demanded.

What if Emmett Jamison was wrong? What if Jason had abducted Lily for the sole purpose of hurting her? What if money wasn't a factor? There would be no reason to keep her alive.

Susan wanted to pound her head against the wall, to shake those horrible thoughts from her brain, but she knew it wouldn't help. Her mind kept straying, betraying her, making the fear worse.

Patrick sat across from her at a glass-topped table in the inner courtyard, sipping decaffeinated coffee. Rosita, the housekeeper, was in the kitchen loading the dishwasher. She'd served a casserole to everyone, including the FBI agents who remained at the house. No one had eaten much, but it had been a "comfort" meal, food for anxious souls.

Susan hadn't spoken to Ethan. She hadn't even seen him. But she knew he'd been sequestered by the feds. The occupants who lived at the Double

Crown weren't permitted to leave their homes, not until the agents completed their interviews. And on top of that, the FBI was taking media-control precautions, making sure that Lily's kidnapping wasn't leaked to the press. Of course family members had been notified, and they'd been worrying themselves sick.

Just like Susan.

"Ryan wants you to stay with your young man tonight," Patrick said.

She glanced up. "What?"

"The veterinarian. Ethan," he added, using the name Ryan must have supplied.

Trying to ease her nerves, she inhaled the nighttime fragrance, the jasmine scenting the air. "Why would he want me to stay there?" she asked, even though she knew. God help her, she knew.

"He seems to think you'll be safer with Ethan." The lights in the inner courtyard cast a warm glow on Patrick's hair: the deep red, the hint of white. He leaned forward, his voice a level above a whisper. "Ryan wants you to have your own special protector."

She closed her eyes, squeezing them shut. How sweet and gallant and sad, she thought. "Ryan feels guilty for not remaining with Lily last night. For going for that walk."

"I know. But what harm can come from you staying with Ethan?"

She opened her eyes. "He's not my lover."

Her uncle sat back, calculating her words. "Yes. Ryan told me. But he already called Ethan and spoke to him about looking after you tonight. And this young man promised that he would respect you." He angled his head. "Do you think he's blowing smoke? Telling Ryan what he wants to hear?"

"No. I think he's being truthful."

"So you trust him?"

"Yes."

"He wouldn't take advantage of you?"

"No."

"Are you as close to him as Ryan thinks you are?"

She thought about the phone call last night, remembering how she'd listened to his voice and imagined his arms locked around her waist. "We're extremely close."

"Then what's wrong with going to him, Susan? With giving Ryan a small measure of peace?"

Her pulse lurched. The idea of spending the night with Ethan warmed her to the bone, but it scared her, too. "He only has one bed."

Patrick shifted in his chair again, creaking the seat. "He already agreed to sleep on the floor. To keep a proper distance between you."

"He did?"

"Yes, but if you don't want to do this, I'll explain it to Ryan. I'll convince him that it's better for you to sleep here."

"No." The word came out before she could stop herself. "I want to stay with Ethan. I've always wanted to be near him, in any way I could. And he's always wanted to protect me."

"Then maybe Ryan is looking after your emotional needs. Both yours and Ethan's."

She gazed across the table at her uncle. His glasses were glaring, shielding his eyes. "I came here to give Ryan comfort, to help him cope with his tumor. But he keeps comforting me instead."

"You're comforting each other. That's what family is for."

"Take care of him tonight. Don't let him keep blaming himself for what happened to Lily."

"I will. But remember that I'm here for you, as well. Call my cell phone if you need anything. Ryan's been using his cell, too. The FBI doesn't want anyone tying up the other lines."

"I'll give Ryan a kiss before I go." She came to her feet, preparing to pack an overnight bag. "Did the FBI interview Ethan yet?"

"Yes. He passed their scrutiny. One of their agents is going to drive you to his house."

"Okay." She took a deep breath and thought

about Lily, about the heartache of being frightened and alone.

A heartache that made Susan want stay with Ethan even more.

Ethan waited on his porch for Susan to arrive, and when the FBI agent dropped her off, he wanted to grab her and never let go. He'd been sitting on pins and needles, waiting to see her, to comfort her, to talk to her about Lily.

Susan exited the agent's car and opened the back door for Chocolate. The dog jumped out and barked, and she walked toward Ethan with a leather satchel over her arm.

He met her at the bottom of the wooden steps and they stood in the yard, as still as stone statues, with Chocolate dancing around them in dizzying circles.

Ethan could see the man behind the steering wheel watching them. Unable to help himself, he reached out to touch Susan's cheek, to feel her skin beneath the tips of his fingers. A connection steeped in fear, in grief, in the beating of their hearts.

Her eyes turned watery, and he sensed that she'd yet to cry, that she'd been hiding her tears before now.

"Let's go inside." He took her bag, relieving her of the cumbersome burden.

"Thank you." She ascended the porch, the dog on her heels.

The FBI operative waited where he was, still keeping an eye on them.

Ethan escorted her into the cabin, resting his hand on the curve of her back. He turned and saw the agent drive away slowly, leaving them alone. Cautious, he locked the door, and the sound of the bolt clicking into place jarred the silence. Chocolate ran to greet the other dogs, wrestling with them, sliding across a small area rug.

"I'm so sorry about Lily," Ethan said.

Susan took an audible breath and blinked away her tears. "They're going to find her. They're going to bring her home. We have to believe that."

"Of course we do." He set her bag on the end table, next to his hat. His heart ached for the rancher who'd lost his wife.

She moved toward the window, her footsteps echoing on the floor. Her face was scrubbed free of makeup, and her hair was secured with barrettes on either side of her face. She looked younger than her thirty-five years, wearing an oversize sweater draped over a pair of jeans.

He realized how awkwardly they were behaving, but this wasn't a casual visit. She had agreed to sleep at his cabin, and he'd promised to keep her safe. He doubted that Jason would come back, not with the feds patrolling the ranch. But he wanted to protect her just the same.

For Ryan.

And for himself.

Silent, he watched her. She remained at the window, looking through the pane of glass. Beyond it, darkness enveloped the ranch.

"I keep wondering where Lily is," she said. "Where Jason took her."

"Me, too." Ethan moved closer, standing beside her, recalling one of his first encounters with Lily. "She gave me an Apache amulet. It was years ago. Soon after she married Ryan."

"Really?" Susan turned to face him. "Why did she give it to you?"

"Because Ryan told her that I had Indian ancestry. Not Apache, though. Another tribe. Comanche. But she gave me the amulet anyway."

Susan seemed intrigued. "Where is it?"

"In storage with most of my other things. I've never worn it." He stalled, tried to explain. "I'm not registered with the tribe or anything like that. It's not something I can claim." And the Native American bloodline had come from his mother's side, something that didn't sit well with him. "It's so minuscule. You know, my great-great-great-somebody was Comanche. Lots of Americans have that kind of Indian blood. It was sweet of

Lily to think of me, but I never understood why it mattered."

She tilted her head. "Maybe she was honoring your great-great-great-somebody. Maybe that mattered to her."

He pressed his palm against the window. "I should get the amulet out of storage and wear it for Lily."

When he dropped his hand, they both turned quiet. The wind had kicked up. He could hear it whistling through the trees, like ghosts leaping off branches, haunting the air. The weather had been strange. Mild one day, brisk the next. He wondered if he should build a fire to keep Susan warm.

"Are you hungry?" he asked. "I can heat up a can of soup."

"I'm fine. Rosita made dinner. But you can eat if you want to."

"I'm fine, too. I was just offering you something." Trying to make her comfortable, to give her the illusion of home. At this point he would do anything to make her feel safe. "I'm glad Ryan asked me to look after you. I'm glad you're here."

"So am I."

The wind made another chilling sound, and she stepped closer to him, letting him be her prince, the man he'd always wanted to be.

"When the FBI interviewed me, I told them I was on the phone with you last night," Ethan said.

"I told them that, too. That I fell asleep."

"I didn't sleep," he admitted. "I was up all night, listening to you. Your breathing was so soft, so…" He let his words fade, realizing how romantic they sounded. "I wish I would have checked on you in person. When I took the phone outside, I counted thirteen stars in the sky. I wasn't sure if that was a bad omen. I'm still wondering if it is."

"Can you imagine how I feel? Knowing that I slept through the kidnapping? I've been telling Ryan not to feel guilty. But what about me? I was in the house when Lily was taken."

"It's not your fault that you didn't wake up."

"I know. But it still hurts."

Giving in to the need to hold her, he took her in his arms. She heaved a battered sigh, clinging to him like a lifeline, burying her face against his shirt.

He stroked her hair, letting the silkiness slip through his fingers. She lifted her head, and their faces were only inches apart. All he had to do was lower his mouth to kiss her.

But he didn't. He couldn't. Not after the promise he'd made to Ryan. The older man hadn't arranged this as a sexual interlude. It was more than that. Something deeper. Stronger. Something that went beyond an affair.

A bit nervous, Ethan wondered if Ryan hoped

that they would fall in love, if he actually thought they were headed in that direction.

He let go of Susan, then glanced at his dusty straw hat, the subtle reminder of who he was. Forever didn't exist, not for a veterinarian from Texas and a psychologist from California. Country boys and city girls didn't mesh, at least not for very long. His parents were proof of that.

An affair, he decided, would be a heck of a lot easier.

"Ethan?"

His pulse thudded in his ears. "Yes?"

"Are you tired?"

"A little," he lied, knowing he probably wouldn't sleep a wink. "Are you?"

She nodded, and he offered to make up their beds, to get the cabin ready.

For the girl of his boyhood dreams to spend the night.

Chapter 8

Susan wasn't as tired as she'd claimed she was, but she thought it would be easier to settle in for the night, to try to relax. Her heart was tripping all over itself, wanting to get closer to Ethan.

Too close, she thought.

He pulled out the sofa bed and put some fresh sheets on it, tucking the clinical white cotton into place. She would have preferred to sleep on sheets that carried his scent. That his body had touched. But he even changed the pillowcase.

Chocolate jumped up on the bed and tried to lie down while Ethan was still in the process of making it, and he shook his head and shooed the dog away. Susan smiled at the persistent Lab. The other dogs were watching him, waiting to see if he was going to defy his master and leap back onto the bed. Chocolate was, without a doubt, the leader of the pack, the wild one of the bunch.

But before he got the chance to impress his canine comrades, Ethan shot him a don't-even-think-about-it glare.

Chocolate gave up and slumped onto the floor, like a kid who wanted to make faces behind his dad's back.

Ethan rolled his eyes and spread a blanket over the top sheet. Susan noticed that it had horseshoes printed on it, sort of like his tattoo, the sexy artwork on his back. Of course she couldn't see his tattoo. His chest wasn't bare.

Suddenly she wondered what he was going to wear to bed. If he would be half-naked.

She'd brought the most conservative sleepwear she owned: a white nightgown with a high-neck collar and lace trim. She'd purchased it at a Victorian-replica flea market, along with a few pieces of furniture she didn't need. But spontaneous shopping sprees were Susan's pamper-herself whim, a female indulgence that sprang from being single.

And lonely, she thought with a grimace.

Ethan glanced at her. He was almost finished making the bed. "Are you okay? Never mind," he added quickly. "Dumb question."

No, it wasn't dumb at all, but she didn't have the courage to admit that she hadn't been thinking about the kidnapping as he probably assumed.

She reached for her bag. "Is it all right if I change in your bathroom?"

"Sure. Go ahead." He folded down the blanket, fussing a bit too much with the bedding.

She went into the cramped bathroom and caught sight of his toiletries on the counter. He used liquid soap, citrus-flavored toothpaste and an electric razor. His aftershave came in a blue bottle, nothing costly, just a drugstore-stocked item that made a simple statement.

Susan refrained from taking a secret whiff, just as she resisted the urge to use his toothpaste. His mouthwash tempted her, too. But she wasn't about to become a this-belongs-to-him thief. Her crush-crazed days were supposed to be over.

Finally she changed into the Victorian-inspired nightgown. Removing the barrettes from her hair, she gazed in the mirror, exhaled a shaky breath and prepared herself for the night ahead.

She entered the other room and saw Chocolate curled up on the bed, looking like the lord of the spoiled-pet manor.

"You gave in," she said to Ethan, who was crouched on the floor, building a fire in a stone hearth. "You let him have his way."

Engrossed in his task, he didn't turn his head,

not even for a quick glance. "I figured he was going to sleep with you anyway."

"What about the other dogs?"

"They'll probably crash with me."

"What are their names?" she asked, realizing she'd never inquired about them.

"Clark and Kent."

"Like Superman?"

He poked at the fire. "Yep."

She sat on the edge of the bed and patted Chocolate's head. He gave her a hyena grin. Clark and Kent were watching Ethan.

The flames, she noticed, sent shades of red dancing across his skin. She could see a hint of his profile, the hard edges and sculpted lines.

He finally turned around. Then froze.

Confused, Susan merely blinked at him.

He jammed his hands in his pockets. "You look like an old-fashioned bride."

Embarrassed, she made a face, scrunching up her nose, wishing she'd thrown on a pair of baggy sweats instead. "It's not supposed to resemble a wedding dress."

He remained where he was, standing in front of the crackling fire, with fragrant timber scenting the air. "I was talking about the honeymoon part. The virgin stuff."

That was even worse, she thought. She was

about as far from virgin as a woman could get. "I guess I overdid it."

"No. I like it." He swept his gaze over her. "I think you look pretty."

"Thank you," she managed, still feeling self-conscious.

"You're welcome," he responded, still checking her out.

Silence drifted like a buoy at sea, and Susan struggled to start a new conversation. But nothing came to mind. Nothing but soundless waves washing over her.

Ethan broke the tension. "I should get my bed ready." He walked across the room, making noise.

Unable to find her voice, she simply watched him from beneath her lashes, trying to keep her anxiety hidden.

He removed a sheepskin throw from the top of the armoire, placed it on the floor and rolled a sleeping bag over it.

That was it. His bed was ready. And it was next to hers, only lower. But he'd chosen the most logical spot. The cabin didn't provide a lot of free-roaming space, so he'd done the best he could, leaving the path to the bathroom open. At least she wouldn't step on him in the middle of the night if her anxious bladder beckoned.

"I'm going to use the head," he told her.

Susan relaxed, realizing his bladder was more

anxious than hers. She tried not to listen, but she heard everything: his practiced aim, the toilet flushing, the faucet running. She even heard him brushing his teeth, using the toothpaste she'd wanted to sample.

If they were lovers, it wouldn't matter. They would be used to the intimacy. But being this close to him, being part of his nighttime ritual, made her feel strangely sexual.

When he came out of the bathroom, she saw that he'd removed his shirt and his boots, but he still wore his jeans. The top snap was undone, creating a slight gap in the material.

If she kissed him, would he taste like citrus?

"Are you ready?" he asked.

She knew he meant for bed. "Yes."

Ethan darkened the cabin, and the fire blazed even brighter, painting him in reddish hues once again.

Susan no longer wondered what he intended to wear. Apparently he'd decided to sleep in his jeans.

While he settled onto the floor, Clark and Kent joined him. Chocolate leaned over the bed and stared at them. Then he jumped down, snuggled next to Ethan and whined at Susan, as if she'd just abandoned him instead of the other way around.

Speaking softly, she tried to soothe the dog, but her calming words only made things worse.

Within no time, he was leaping up and down, between her and Ethan, frantic about where to sleep.

"I don't think this is going to work," she said.

Ethan sat up and dragged his hand through his hair. "I'll put him outside."

"Don't do that. It's windy out there." She sat up, too, a sudden chill racking her bones. Lily's kidnapping came back full force, and she gulped the air in her lungs, imagining her in a dark, dank place. "Please, Ethan, let him stay."

"And sleep where?"

She rocked forward, hugging herself, but the dark and dank image wouldn't go away. "With us."

His voice turned rough. "You mean together?"

Chocolate was still doing his neurotic dance, leaping from bed to sleeping bag. "Yes."

"I promised Ryan I'd keep a proper distance between us."

She looked at Ethan and felt her heart stumble. The flames created a halo effect, making his skin glow. His knees were drawn to his chest, and she realized he was hugging himself, too. "Three dogs is a proper distance," she said. "Clark and Kent can sleep with us, too."

He blew out a ragged breath. "I feel like I'm betraying Ryan."

"But you're not. He asked you to protect me, and you will be." She needed him next to her, close to her. "I want to reach out and know you're there."

"Is that honestly how you feel?" He stood, then sat on the edge of the bed so they could talk face-to-face, so they could look into each other's fire-lit eyes. "You're not just doing this for Chocolate?"

She touched his hand. "No. It's for us, too."

His fingers found hers. "I've never slept with a woman and not had sex with her."

She almost laughed, almost cried, almost pulled him down on top of her. "There's nothing wrong with cuddling. It will be good for you."

"Then I better get under the covers." He smiled, motioned to her canine bedmate. "Like he did." By now Chocolate had cemented himself to Susan, aware, it seemed, that his "parents" were going to stay together.

She made room for Ethan and he slid next to her, taking her in his arms. She couldn't imagine a safer place to be. She could feel the rise and fall of his chest, the warmth of his body, the raw, rugged strength of his embrace. She pressed her lips against his shoulder, and he ran his hand along her back, along her old-fashioned nightgown. For one crazy instant, she actually felt like a virgin bride.

He called the other two dogs, and they leaped onto the bed and nudged their way into the coziness. Chocolate was already snoring, with his butt in the air.

Susan closed her eyes, grateful for the tall, dark angel Ryan had given her. For Ethan Eldridge, the honor-bound boy who'd grown into an honor-bound man.

"Will you say a prayer with me?" she whispered, opening her eyes and watching the fire.

"Of course I will." He held her even closer, and together they spoke to the Creator.

Asking Him to keep Lily safe, to bring her home, to reunite her with her husband.

Darkness surrounded her, looming like monsters, invisible creatures breathing down the sides of her neck. Lily squinted, but she couldn't see through the blindfold, not even the slightest hint of light.

How long had she been gone? A few hours? A full day? She couldn't remember how many times Jason had drugged her. She'd been drifting in and out of consciousness, waiting for the monsters to strike.

She had no idea where she was. The ground was uneven and the surface beneath her back seemed bumpy.

She listened for background noise, but nothing stirred. Her hands and feet were bound, and a rough cloth, a gag, cut into the sides of her mouth. She wanted to wet her lips, but she couldn't.

Images of Ryan swirled in her fog-enshrouded mind. Memories. Photos she couldn't touch. The man she loved.

Footsteps sounded, and she stiffened, chills crawling up her spine.

Jason had returned.

"Lily, my love."

The familiar greeting brought bile to her throat. But she couldn't vomit. She couldn't purge this nightmare.

He'd touched her earlier, running his hands all over her body, like thousands of poisonous spiders spinning a web. He hadn't raped her, but she feared he would.

Suddenly she heard a small click, then smelled the scent of burning tobacco. He'd just lit a cigarette.

His lighter clicked again—the metal lid snapping shut. "Are you scared of me?" he asked.

She didn't react. Nothing. No movement. She would rather die than admit how afraid she was.

"I'm holding a lantern up to your face. I can see you, Mrs. Fortune. Don't you wish you could see me?"

Mrs. Fortune. She tried to envision her wedding day, to escape in Ryan's arms.

"Do you know how much I want to hurt you?"

Beneath the blindfold, she squeezed her eyelids, closing them even more, trying to block out his voice.

"This much," he said, burning her arm with the cigarette.

She flinched from the pain, from the searing of flesh.

"That's my girl. Show me how much it hurts."

He did it again. Then he kissed her, right over the gag. She could feel his face pressed against hers.

The bile in her throat returned.

"I'll be back in the morning," he said, pulling away, chuckling to himself. "But for now you need to sleep." He tucked a blanket around her. "Bad dreams, Lily."

When he covered her nose with a chemical-doused rag, drugging her once again, she breathed deeply, welcoming the slumber, praying that morning would never come.

Ethan awakened at the crack of dawn, but the rest of his family—for lack of a better word—was still asleep. Susan's body was pressed close to his. Incredibly close, he thought. So close, her face was buried against his chest. He could feel her breath rippling across his skin, stimulating his nipples.

Chocolate was on the other side of her, with his head propped against her hip. He'd even drooled on her nightgown. Clark and Kent were curled into two furry balls, relying on each other for warmth.

Ethan moved his arm and wrapped it around Susan. He wanted to lift her chin and kiss her, to fill his senses with a blast of tongue-tangling heat.

Cuddling was nice, damn sweet, but it wasn't the same as…

Chocolate opened his eyes and squinted at him, catching him in a sexual thought.

He squinted right back. The dog had no room to talk. None whatsoever. He'd stuck his nose in Susan's crotch on the first day he'd met her. Ethan hadn't even gotten to first base.

She made a slow, soft, moaning sound and his body reacted, electrifying the teeth on his zipper.

Thank goodness Chocolate had gone back to sleep. He wanted to enjoy this moment without feeling guilty.

Of course that was wishful thinking. His promise to Ryan weighed heavily on his mind.

Slipping out of bed, he eased away from Susan. The lost contact almost made him shiver. But the cabin was cold. The fire had burned out, leaving nothing but charred wood.

He went into the bathroom to splash some water on his face and brush his teeth. Susan had left her overnight bag on top of the hamper, a reminder that she was only staying for one day. He wondered what Ryan would say if he asked the older man for permission to keep her until Lily came home.

When he returned to the living room, Susan was awake, sitting up in bed, gazing at the empty hearth. He knew she was thinking about Lily. He could see the sadness in her eyes.

"It will be okay," he said.

She shifted her gaze, looking directly at him, making his heart pound. He wanted to climb back into bed and hold her all over again, to try to take away the pain.

She clutched her pillow. "I keep telling myself that it will be okay. But then I think about Jason and the awful things he's done." Her breath hitched. "What if Ryan dies without ever seeing Lily again? What if she's lost forever?"

Ethan didn't know what to say. He wasn't a grief counselor. Although Susan probably had that kind of training, she was too close to the situation to comfort herself.

"Our prayers are going to work," he finally said. "They have to. Ryan and Lily need each other."

She gave him a small smile, thanking him for the comfort. "You're a good man, Ethan."

He smiled, too. "You wouldn't say that if you knew what I'd been thinking about when I first woke up."

"I can only imagine."

She threw her pillow at him, and he caught it and tossed it back at her. All three dogs stirred, wondering what the heck the grown-ups were doing.

"I'll fix you some breakfast," Ethan said.

"Cereal and milk?"

"How'd you guess?"

"You're a bachelor."

"Not today. I've got you and the kids."

"You've always got the kids. You're a single dad." She smoothed her prim and proper nightgown. "Is it all right if I take a shower before breakfast?"

"Sure." He couldn't help but grin. "Want some company?"

She threw the pillow at him again, and they both laughed. He was glad he'd been able to lighten her mood. It made him feel like the protector Ryan had called upon him to be. He decided to leave the bed as it was, a reminder that she'd spent the night with him.

While she bathed, he let the dogs out and brewed a pot of coffee. Then he placed the little sugar and creamer packets on the counter. Next he took inventory of his cereal, hoping she liked the nonfrosted kind.

Twenty minutes later she emerged from the bathroom, looking like a Texas mermaid, with damp hair, a seashell-printed T-shirt and slim-fitting jeans.

She met him in the kitchen. "The coffee smells good."

Ethan poured her a cup, and as she doctored the heavy dark brew, he leaned over to smell her hair. Apparently she'd brought her own shampoo. The scent of lemons drifted to his nostrils like a sun-warmed orchard.

"What are you doing?" she asked.

"Nothing." He stepped back, nearly bumping his head on a cabinet.

"Were you looking down my shirt?"

"What? No." He wouldn't dare admit that he'd been sniffing her hair. That sounded more perverted than peering down her top. "Are you hungry? How about that cereal?"

"Very clever. Changing the subject." She scolded him with a teasing look. "But I'll take a bowl of whatever you're having."

They ate in front of the TV, on the unmade bed, and Ethan switched channels with the remote control, waiting to see what sparked Susan's interest. She reacted to a vintage cartoon, where Wile E. Coyote had just ignited a stick of dynamite.

She smiled at the screen. "I used to watch this when I was a kid."

"Me, too." As Road Runner beep-beeped his way past the singed and scorched coyote, Ethan remembered how his mom used to plunk him in front of the TV and ignore him for the rest of the day. Even as a boy, he knew the difference between the kinds of moms his friends had and the one fate had given him.

He cleared his mind, refusing to continue his walk down memory lane, to let it consume him. His dad had spent too many years traveling that shaky road, obsessing about his ex-wife.

He looked at Susan and wondered if she would ever get married, or if her career would keep getting in the way. At least she was honest with herself. She didn't pretend to be something she wasn't.

She turned and looked at him, too. And for a moment they stared at each other. They were only a heartbeat away from a kiss, from letting their emotions go.

But they didn't. She broke eye contact, and they gazed at the TV as if their lives depended on a cartoon.

When the program ended, she reached for their bowls. "I'll do the dishes."

"Don't worry about it." He'd left plates and silverware in the sink from previous meals, but he'd become accustomed to the clutter. "I can deal with it later."

"I don't mind. I like to keep busy."

So did he, but not with housework. A trait he must have inherited from his nondomestic mom.

Susan insisted on tidying up the kitchen, so Ethan decided to take a shower, to clear his senses.

Standing in the narrow stall, he let the water pummel him, hitting his body like a fast-driving rain.

Afterward he realized that he'd forgotten to bring clean clothes into the bathroom. He dried off, then wrapped a towel around his waist.

When he entered the main room, he walked over to the armoire. Susan was still in the kitchen. "Don't come in here," he called out. "I'm getting dressed."

"I can't even sneak one little peek?" she called back.

By now she was scrubbing his stove. He could see her, but her back was turned. She couldn't see him.

He grinned and dropped his towel, knowing damn well she wasn't going to turn around. "It would be more like a big peek," he told her, wondering if she would catch the double entendre.

She did. Immediately. "How big?"

He chuckled and slipped on a pair of boxers. It felt good to flirt, to combat their attraction with humor. *"Mucho, mucho grande,"* he said, and heard her laugh.

"You wish."

"Feels like it when I'm around you." He zipped into a pair of threadbare jeans and pulled a plain white T-shirt over his head. "I'm decent now."

"Then I'll be there in a minute."

Since she decided to finish cleaning the stove, he opened the front door and stood on the porch, checking on the dogs. They were romping through the grass, having a high ole time.

The phone rang, sending Ethan back inside. The man on the other end of the line announced who he was.

Special Agent Jamison. Jason's FBI brother.

His pulse raced. "Is this about Lily?"

"Yes, it is. Ryan asked me to call, to give you an update. An audiotape arrived at the house this morning with a message from Jason. He claimed Lily is alive, but he refuses to offer proof."

"Did he say anything else?"

"He requested a ransom, but he didn't arrange for a drop-off. He's supposed to send a second tape to the house with more information."

"When?"

"He didn't specify."

Ethan glanced at Susan. She was no longer in the kitchen. She'd caught wind of his conversation and was coming toward him. "So all he did is give Ryan a chance to gather the money?"

"That's right."

"How is Ryan?" Ethan asked. "Is he holding up okay?"

"He's doing the best he can, under the circumstances. He's with Patrick. They're on their way to Fortune-Rockwell to get the cash. An agent is with them, as well."

When the call ended, Ethan reached for Susan's hand. She looked into his eyes and he filled her in, repeating what Emmett had said. Then he asked her to go to the storage facility with him.

And search for the amulet that had once belonged to Lily.

Chapter 9

Security was still tight. No one on the ranch could go anywhere without checking with the FBI first, which, of course, Susan and Ethan had done.

So here they were, getting ready to tackle their quest. She couldn't see beyond the boxes that were stacked above her head. She waited on the sidelines while Ethan brought some down to her level. But she didn't mind. She understood his urgency, his need to find the amulet.

Especially today.

In spite of Jason's claim, they had no way of knowing that Lily was still alive. They were running on hope, on fear, on emotions that tangled like vines.

She stood, with her back to the sun, recalling the wind that had howled throughout the night. The weather had softened, giving way to a mild breeze.

"Do you remember where you put the amulet?" she asked. "What was marked on the outside of the box?"

"It should say 'bedroom,' but there are lots of those. I'm trying to find all of them." He heaved another heavy load. "I wasn't very organized when I was packing."

Susan glanced at the pile he'd separated. "Is it okay if I get started?"

"Sure. Go ahead." He stopped for a moment, then adjusted his hat, pushing the brim up and revealing his eyes.

They were exceptionally blue, she noticed. A stark contrast to his tanned skin. If she looked deep enough, she might be able to see the Indian in him, but she knew that didn't matter. This wasn't about his distant ancestors. This was about Lily and the gift she'd given him.

Susan used Ethan's pocketknife, opening the first box, then realized she had no idea what she was searching for. "What does the amulet look like?"

"It's small," he responded. "A piece of pine,

shaved very thin and carved, a bit roughly, into the shape of a person." He paused, making a thoughtful expression. "But you won't be able to tell if it's male or female. The only distinguishing marks are lines that represent lightning."

She glanced up. "Are they painted on?"

"No. They're incised in the wood. I wouldn't have known what they stood for if Lily hadn't told me." He found another "bedroom" box and placed it beside her. "The charm is supposed to have special power. Lily said that Apache men and women used to wear them. Children, too. They even tied them onto their babies' cradle boards."

Susan sighed, her voice fading in the breeze. "I wish Lily had been wearing one."

"Me, too. But maybe if I start wearing it, it will transcend to her." He frowned, as if he'd never been superstitious before now.

Of course, neither had she. She relied on logic, on a library of textbooks, on psychological theories. But she relied on empathy, too. On trying to heal the human psyche.

"If you believe it will help protect Lily, then it will," she said.

He smiled, thanking her without words, without making a sound. Suddenly her heart did a demonstrative flip, an Olympic-size somersault right to her throat. She wanted to kiss him, to put her mouth against his, to comfort the ache in both of their souls.

Time seemed to stop, like a thousand clocks suspended in space, refusing to tick, to advance to the next second.

She looked at her watch, just to be sure, and he turned away, resuming his work.

When every ounce of air in her lungs whooshed out, she decided, right then and there, that she was going to make love with him.

Tonight, she thought. In the shelter of his cabin.

Anxious, she shifted the knife in her hand and saw the blade flash in the sun. Should she say something to him? Admit that she was going to...

Going to what? Seduce him? It wasn't as if he hadn't made his hunger clear.

Not that he looked particularly lustful now. He was concentrating on finding the amulet, the way she should be doing.

She set down the knife and sorted through the first box, discovering a hodgepodge of items. Most of the contents were coats and jackets, but she came across a few books, some worn-out boots and a Western hat tin. She studied it, assuming it was an airplane carry-on, something a man like Ethan would consider a vital part of his luggage.

The next box was just as jumbled: more old clothes, a portable CD player, a collection of silver snuffboxes that had probably belonged to his father. From what she recalled, his dad had chewed tobacco.

She wondered if he'd kept anything that had belonged to his mother, if he was sentimental about her. When they were teenagers, Susan had asked him about his mom, and he'd told her that she'd been gone a long time. Gone meant dead, or so she assumed. To her, his father had always seemed like a widower, a tough yet tender ranch hand who'd secretly grieved for his dead wife. At the time Ethan's family had seemed sadly poetic, filling her imagination with hearts and flowers.

Steeped in memories, in the crush that had fueled her youth, Susan looked up at him. He was wiping his hands on his pants. Everything in his storage unit had been locked away for several months, gathering dust, collecting residue from a sixty-day escrow that had yet to close.

She slid her gaze down the length of his jeans, where the seams frayed. A horizontal-shaped hole formed at one knee, white threads stretching across the fabric. Even the material around his fly was beginning to wear.

Lost in the moment, she stared at his zipper, at the slight ridge that—

"Susan?"

She teetered on her feet, blinked, readjusted her gaze. "What?"

"Any luck?"

"No. Not yet. Did you find all the 'bedroom' boxes?"

"I think so." He picked up the pocketknife and sliced the seal on the cardboard container in front of him.

She watched him, her skin a bit too warm. Was she getting in over her head? Would being intimate with him make her long for more? For something deeper? Or would she be able to adopt his attitude and take in stride the affair he'd been campaigning for?

Why not? she asked herself. She wasn't a desperate teenager anymore, substituting sex for love. She knew the difference.

"I found it." He lifted the amulet, dangling the leather cord in his hand.

Susan moved closer, checking out the necklace. It fit his description, right down to the tiniest detail. Curious, she touched the charm, tracing the carved form.

"It's made from wood that was struck by lightning," he said. "That's what makes it so valuable to the Apache."

"I wonder how old it is." She studied incisions, the decorative lines that gave the primitive amulet an artistic quality.

"I have no idea." He waited a beat, then slipped it over his head.

She could tell that he was barely breathing.

Susan held her breath, too. The necklace fell against his shirt like an idol god.

The charm looked right on him, she thought. Strong. Potent. As chiseled as his features, as rough as the unshaven texture of his skin.

She wanted to put her hands all over him, but she didn't. Instead she reached for the tape they'd brought, closing the boxes they'd opened, thinking about the promise she'd made to herself.

To make love without getting attached.

The day had gone from mild to gloomy, creating an overcast hue in Ryan and Lily's bedroom.

Susan joined her cousin in the sitting area, taking the spot next to him on the sofa. He'd returned from Fortune-Rockwell with the ransom in tow. For now it was in a floor safe, waiting for Jason's next instructions to arrive.

"The FBI doesn't think he's going to contact me again until tomorrow," Ryan said. "Or maybe even the day after."

She looked at his disheveled appearance, the way he'd ransacked his hair and skewed his shirt. Making the Fortune patriarch agonize over his wife was part of the kidnapper's ploy. "I know. I'm sorry."

"He didn't even let me hear her voice. Am I supposed to trust him that she's still alive?"

"Yes, you are." Susan leaned her head against

his shoulder, giving him the comfort of human contact, of family. "You have to stay strong for Lily. We all do."

"I'm trying. I swear I am." He put his arms around her, holding on to her like a lifeline.

They stayed like that, silent, connected, giving each other hope. She thought about the amulet, praying that Ethan's attempt to help protect Lily was working.

Finally Ryan let go, his chest heaving with a labored breath. She could see how exhausted he was. In between bouts of tears and the ever-constant fear, he was still fighting a brain tumor.

"The FBI is analyzing the tape at their forensic audio lab," Ryan said. "Trying to identify background noises, trying to figure out where Jason was when he recorded it. In a house, in a car, outside somewhere." He paused, his voice cracking. "They're searching for signs of Lily on the tape, too."

"If she was breathing in the background?"

He cleared his throat. "Yes."

Susan looked at the fireplace and noticed a picture of Lily on the mantel. An unframed photograph that depicted her when she was a teenager, a snapshot Ryan had removed from one of Lily's photo albums and placed there.

"What about the envelope the tape arrived in?" she asked. "The FBI must be analyzing that, too."

"They are, and they know that Jason used a courier service in Houston and that he was in disguise. But he won't go back to the same city next time or use the same disguise."

"What about Lily's truck?"

"They think he's been changing the plates, doing whatever he can to camouflage it. But for the most part he's been lying low, hiding out somewhere." Ryan shifted on the couch, grabbing the decorative pillow on the other side of him. "He insisted on hundred-dollar bills."

"What?" The change of topic jarred her.

"That's the ransom. Two million in hundred-dollar bills. The FBI says he chose larger bills because the money weighs less that way."

"Light enough for him to carry?"

Ryan nodded. "He wants the cash divided into two duffel bags. All those damn demands. No consecutive serial numbers, no marked bills, no new bills, no tracking devices." His voice cracked again. "All I care about is getting my wife back."

"I know. Me, too." She glanced at Lily's teenage photograph, at her long raven hair and dark eyes. "I can see why you fell in love with her."

"Those days were bittersweet."

"Young love always is."

He turned to face her, tilting his head, studying her. She sensed he was going to change the subject, direct the conversation toward her.

And Ethan.

"Where's your young man?" he asked, right on cue.

"I was with him this morning, but he's working now, examining a bull the foreman wants to purchase. Doing a semen check and all that."

"Are you going to see him later?"

She nodded, inhaled a gust of air into her lungs. "I'd like to stay with him again tonight."

"That's fine. I'd feel better knowing that he's looking after you."

"I know, but—"

His eyes questioned her. "But what?"

She took another deep breath, preparing for the impact of saying it out loud. "I want to get romantic with him this time."

Ryan sat back, mulling over her words. She recognized his paternal look, the care and concern he'd always expressed for her. "Are you asking for my permission?"

"No. I just wanted you to be aware of my decision." Susan shifted in her seat. She still hadn't told Ethan about her plans, yet she'd spilled her gabby-girl guts to Ryan.

He took her hand, holding it gently in his. "I've always wanted you and Ethan to get together. I've always thought he would be the perfect mate for you."

A mate, she thought. A long-term relationship. Ryan was thinking with his heart. "I'm not talking about love."

"Of course you are."

"No." She snared his gaze, imploring him to understand. "I'm not."

"Hogwash." He made a determined face, like a sweet, stubborn old goat. "Sooner or later you two are going to be walking down the aisle."

"That's not going to happen, Ryan."

"Yes, it is." He refused to take no for answer, to dismantle the castle he'd just built. "And I know darn well Lily would agree with me."

Susan sighed. She couldn't keep challenging him, not now, not like this. Not after he'd brought Lily into it.

Unsure of what else to do, she put her head on his shoulder again, letting him know that she was still his, the little girl who adored him.

He wrapped his arms around her, returning her affection. "I won," he said.

Yes, Susan thought. But only by default.

"You're going to marry him someday. I can feel it."

She let him keep his fairy tale. Then she closed her eyes and wondered if he was planning her nonexistent wedding in his mind, envisioning himself and Lily by her side.

* * *

Lily awakened from a dream that had kept her safe, with Ryan holding her close. And then darkness swarmed over her, the reality of where she was.

Tears clogged her eyes, burning behind the blindfold. The blanket draped over her body smelled like Jason. Cigarette smoke clung to it, the odor making her stomach roil.

She did her best to knock it away, even if she couldn't use her hands. She wasn't cold. The walls and the floor seemed irregular, like rocks and gravel. But the air was clean and the temperature constant. If she were outside, wouldn't the weather change? Wouldn't there be sounds from nature? Crickets chirping at night? Birds singing in the morning?

Every so often she thought she heard a faucet dripping, but that made no sense. Wherever she was, there was no indoor plumbing. Jason had forced her to use a bedpan or some sort of portable device. Much to her humiliation, he'd removed her underwear, baiting her with crude remarks, leaving her naked beneath her nightgown.

Lily's body ached and her lips were parched, but Jason had only been giving her sparing sips of water. And on top of everything else, the binding around her hands and wrists felt like iron.

If she rubbed the rope against the wall behind her, would it fray?

With her heart thudding in her ears, she tried it. But all she could feel was the pain of her skin being scraped against a rough-hewn surface.

She winced, stopped the process and wished that everything wasn't so dark. She hated being blindfolded. She had no sense of place, no sense of time.

Was it morning? Or had she slept through the afternoon? Either way, she sensed that Jason wasn't coming back for a while. That he'd gotten sidetracked somewhere, leaving her alone.

Grateful that he wasn't nearby, she started rubbing her wrists against the wall again. She didn't care if she scraped every ounce of flesh off her arms. She had to cut through the rope. She had to get away.

And escape the demon that had kidnapped her.

Déjà vu, Ethan thought.

He stood on his porch, a late-day breeze blowing his hair across his eyes. Susan arrived in a white sedan chauffeured by the same FBI agent who'd driven her to his house the night before.

She climbed out of the passenger seat, and the driver kept the car running. Was he waiting for her to collect her overnight bag she'd left in Ethan's bathroom?

He'd meant to call Ryan and ask if she could stay with him again, but he hadn't gotten the chance. After work, he'd come home, grabbed a beer and let the dogs out.

Then she'd showed up.

He noticed that she carried an oversize purse and her hair was tucked behind her ears. Unlike him, she wasn't wearing the same clothes she'd put on that morning. Instead, she'd changed into a stretchy pink top and wore sugary lipstick to match.

He wondered if she would taste like bubble gum. Or cotton candy. Or that sweet, decadent frosting the bakery put on their Valentine's Day cakes.

Chocolate ran to greet her, and Ethan contemplated the upcoming holiday. Should he buy her something? Or would that be pushing the boundaries of their relationship, of the friend-only agreement they'd made?

She ruffled the dog's fur, then looked up and caught Ethan's gaze. He pulled on his beer, taking a long, thirst-quenching drink.

When she approached him, he tried to act casual. "Are you here to get your stuff?" He waited a second. "Or to stay another night?"

"To stay." She chewed her bottom lip, pulling the frosted pink color against her teeth. "If you don't mind."

Was she kidding? "Of course I don't mind." He sat on one of the creaky wooden steps, inviting her to join him.

She did, right before she signaled the federal agent, letting him know that he was free to go.

The car crept past the cabin and onto a back road. Ethan watched it disappear. "Did you really think I would turn you away?"

"No, but it doesn't hurt to ask and…" She stalled, started over. "And it was my idea this time, not Ryan's."

"Really?" He thought about Valentine's Day again, about buying her a gift. Then he glanced at the dogs, grateful they were amusing themselves instead of demanding Susan's attention.

She shifted in her seat. "Ryan thinks we're going to fall in love, get married, the whole bit."

He made a twisted face. "I suspected that Ryan felt that way."

"You did?"

"Yeah. Didn't you?"

"He's been prodding me from the beginning. Teasing me about you. But I didn't expect him to bring up marriage, to be so convinced it's going to happen."

He took a swig of his beer, then, a bit remiss, he offered the bottled draft to her. He hadn't meant to be a lousy host. When she declined the drink, he asked, "Did you set him straight?"

"I tried, but he refused to listen."

Ethan gazed at the Fortune land, at the scatter of prairie grass, the wild shrubs and historic oaks that surrounded the cabin. There was no point in being angry with Ryan for wanting to find Susan a husband. The older man was battling for his own happily-ever-after. "His intentions are misguided, but he means well."

"That's why I dropped it. Why I didn't keep pressing the issue. But it was probably my fault to begin with—" She fumbled, nearly knocking her too-big purse off the step. "Considering what I told him."

He frowned at her. "What do you mean? What are you talking about?"

"You know."

No, he didn't. "You've lost me."

This time she grabbed the bottle. "I want to have sex with you, Ethan."

Silence. Two hearts pounding at the speed of light.

"Damn." It was the only thing he could think of to say, the only response that popped into his befuddled brain. But it was a good damn. Damn good. "When?" he asked.

"Tonight." She gulped the beer, putting her mouth where his had been.

He watched her. And got aroused. "Are you sure you want to be with me? Are you absolutely sure?"

She nodded, took another drink, swallowed.

He got even more turned-on, hard and hot and anxious. But he couldn't give in. Not yet. "What about you not having affairs anymore? What about all that stuff you told me?"

"It's not as if I'll be sleeping with a stranger. You're my friend. My old crush. The boy I always wanted." She returned the beer. "But that doesn't mean I'm going to fall in love with you. I know the difference. I can handle it."

"So can I." Every fantasy he'd dared to dream about her was spinning in his mind.

Like cotton candy and bubble gum and Valentine icing.

He stood, helped her up. He would go crazy if he had to wait until tonight. "Let's go inside."

She teetered on her feet. "You're making me dizzy. Tingly all over."

"Good." He pulled her into his arms, determined to hold her, to romance her, to peel off her clothes.

One sweet layer at a time.

Chapter 10

Susan scrambled for her purse.

"What's in there?" Ethan asked. "What's so important?"

She latched on to the leather handle. "Condoms."

He grinned and spun her around. "How many boxes?"

"A lot." Too many, she thought. But she wanted to be prepared, for as long as they were going to be lovers, for as long as their affair lasted.

He yanked her tight against him, and she could feel muscles bunching beneath his T-shirt. And his jeans, those frayed denims, proved how strong and solid and aroused he was.

He closed the cabin door, locking them inside. She let go of her purse and noticed the sofa was pulled out, made into a bed, leftover from last night. She liked that he'd kept it that way.

But a moment later fear shot through her blood, making her shiver. Was she deceiving herself? Going back in time and becoming the old Susan?

He touched her cheek, let his hand linger. "What's wrong?"

"I have this urge to be wild. To do all sorts of crazy things to you. But it scares me, too."

"You shouldn't repress your feelings, Susan."

Memories assaulted her brain. "But I've worked so hard to be good."

"This is different. You're not the troubled girl you used to be, and I'm not one of those other boys." He leaned into her. "I've fantasized about you being wild for me. But I would never disrespect you for it. Not then and not now." He rubbed his thumb across her lips, smearing her lipstick, just a little, just enough to make her heart catch. "I've craved you for over half my life."

"Me, too."

"Then let it happen." He kissed her. The kiss they'd been waiting for. Seventeen years of pent-up lust, of boy-girl hunger, of the most incredible feeling in the world.

He tasted like sex and sin and warm saliva. His tongue swirled with hers, meeting, mating, making her limbs weak.

She gripped his shoulders, and he pulled her even closer, cupping her bottom, dragging her hips against his, creating friction, the way he'd probably wanted to do when they were young.

Innocent, dangerous foreplay, she thought.

One quick breath, one gust of air and they kissed all over again.

She kicked off her shoes, a pair of strappy sandals that slid across the floor. He got rid of his boots, too, stumbling to keep her in his arms, to not let go.

Hands questing, she toyed with his belt buckle, slipping lower, brushing his fly. He nibbled her neck, using his teeth, sucking and biting. She gave him free rein, hoping he left marks on her skin.

He stepped back, looked at her. "I want to take off your clothes. I want to see your bra, your panties, what you wore for me."

He lifted the Lycra fabric, and she raised her arms, letting him undress her. The material was tight, making it difficult for him to strip it away. But she could tell he enjoyed the challenge.

"It's pink," he said the moment her bra was exposed. He yanked off her shirt, tossing it onto the floor. "Pretty poison. Pretty pink." He tugged at the lace cups, pushing them down, making her nipples pop out.

She knew what came next. He was going to lick her like a lollipop. His candy. His poison.

Susan braced herself. How many times had she imagined this? Ethan Eldridge touching her? Teasing her?

He lowered his head, and she delved into his hair.

He licked; he sucked; he drove her half-mad. She pitched forward, pushing her nipple farther into his mouth.

"It hurts," she said.

He glanced up. "A good hurt?"

"Yes." She watched him switch sides. "Do it harder."

That made him smile. "How hard?"

"As hard as you can."

He went after her like a rabid animal, sucking with a vengeance. When he was through, her nipples were raw and swollen, aching and throbbing.

Dizzy, she bit her lip, loving every second of it. He dropped to his knees and tugged on her jeans, dragging them down her hips. When he got to her underwear, a pair of panties that matched her bra, he played with the elastic band.

"Show me," he said.

She knew what he meant. He wanted her to pull them down, right there, right in front of his face.

Her skin went warm, a blush that heated every inch of her body. But she did what he asked her to do, excited by his request, by the wickedness that came over her.

Needing more, she moved closer to his mouth. "Is this what you want?"

"Yes." He parted her with his thumbs. "I can't believe this is happening." He darted his tongue, making her quiver. "You're as wild as I imagined."

And he was grazing her thighs, abrading her with his beard stubble. She touched his face, tracing those rugged features.

He glanced up, shocking her with his eyes, with how powerfully blue they were.

She watched what he did to her. She even rocked back and forth, encouraging him, showing him what she liked. The roughness. The softness.

He took his time, bathing her in sensation, in wetness, in butterfly kisses that nearly cracked her soul.

And then it happened. Pleasure poured over her, like a jar of wax, as bright and blue and feverish as his eyes. She'd never felt so treasured.

"Ethan." She said his name, and he lifted her up and carried her to bed, where they tumbled onto the sheets.

And into the luxury of each other's arms.

* * *

Ethan nuzzled the side of her neck, breathing in the scent of her hair. He could still taste her, and the flavor sent shock waves through his veins, rippling beneath his skin.

"You almost made me come," he said.

"Really?"

"Uh-huh."

"Can I see?" She sketched her hand along the waistband of his jeans.

"You gotta get me naked first."

"No problem." She removed his shirt, and while she undid his belt, he lifted his hips.

His pants came next, his boxers, his socks. She didn't waste any time. She stripped him to the bone. The only article that remained was the Apache amulet around his neck. But that wasn't what caught her attention. She stared at his erection, where moisture seeped at the tip.

"I told you," he said.

"So you did." She collected the pearly drop with her finger. Then brought it to his lips, daring him to taste it.

Properly stunned, he shook his head, laughed, hoped she wasn't serious. She wasn't. She sucked on her own finger instead, taking what she'd offered to him. Ethan watched her, and the sound, the motion, the knowledge of what she was doing made another bead of semen appear.

This time he wanted her to put her mouth on it.

But she didn't. She lowered her head and kissed his stomach, purposely missing her mark.

His muscles jumped, creating a rippling effect. He considered nudging her farther down, but he decided to wait, to let her seduce him.

She looked up and smiled, and he held his breath. Dusk slipped through the blinds, casting shadows across the bed, draping her in soft, wintry colors.

He combed his fingers through her hair, and she licked his belly button, nearly bringing his craving to fruition.

Finally, she stroked him, using her hands, positioning him against her lips, getting him ready, making him even more aroused than he already was.

He closed his eyes, just for a moment, just for one life-altering second. And in the silence, in the stillness, she took him in her mouth.

Deep, hard, thrilling. He couldn't get enough.

Slipping under her spell, he caressed her face, her shoulders, every part of her he could reach.

Finally, before he exploded, before he lost control, he pulled her up, where they kissed like reckless lovers, refusing to let go.

She straddled his lap. "I warned you that I felt like being wild."

And he knew that he would like it. That he

would crave her even more. He lunged forward and caught her in another kiss. She was as addictive as a drug. "I used to think about you when I—" He stalled, realized what he was about to say.

"I know, Ethan. I used to do that, too."

Her admission made him shudder. "No one's ever said that to me before."

"I wasn't just saying it. It's true."

"I believe you." He knew how important he'd always been to her. And he wished that those other boys hadn't hurt her. That he could have kept the wolves at bay.

Her eyes turned watery, and he brought her against his chest, giving her the solace they both needed.

"I should have saved you," he said.

She blinked away her sadness, kissing him softly. "You're doing it now."

He smiled, nipped her jaw, latched on to her hips. "Are you ready?"

"Yes. More than ready."

"Then I want to be on top."

She laughed and rolled over. "Men and their power trips." Her hand crawled up his thigh. "We need a condom."

"Yours or mine?" He had a supply in the armoire and another batch in a bathroom drawer, probably as many as she'd stuffed in her purse.

"Whose is closer?"

"I think it's a draw."

"One of each?" she suggested.

He lifted his eyebrows. "I'm not wearing two."

She lunged for her purse. "I was kidding."

Like kids in a candy store, they dug through her bag, choosing an ultrathin style. He tore it open and watched her roll it over every anxious inch.

"You're good at that," he said, grateful that the protection had become part of their foreplay. "I used to hate this part."

"But now you like it?"

"I like everything with you." He slid his fingers through hers, holding her hands above her head, pinning her beneath his body. "Everything."

She wet her lips. "Me, too."

"Will you move in with me?" he asked, the question rising like a volcano. He couldn't have stopped it if he tried.

Her eyes went wide. "For how long?"

"For as long as you're in Texas."

"Yes. Absolutely."

He kissed her, using his tongue, his teeth, his entire mouth. They both knew that his invitation, their upcoming living arrangement, was only temporary.

But it was enough, he thought. All they needed to feel secure, to explore their relationship without drowning.

She wrapped her legs around him, and he entered her, to the hilt, as deep as he could go.

In the next instant they went crazy, beautifully insane. He filled her perfectly, the way a man should fill a woman. Moist heat surrounded him, clutching, drawing him closer.

He moved; she moved with him, rolling over the bed, keeping him locked between her legs. Lust roared in his head, pounding with every stroke, with every glorious thrust.

Her lashes fluttered, soft and silky and desperately erotic. He wondered why he'd ever slept with anyone else. She was it. His fantasy. His dream.

They made love at a dizzying pace, in a tangle of limbs, in voracious pants, in carnal images careening through his mind. And when she bucked beneath him, when she came all over him, he breathed her name.

Then took his own mindless fall.

While Ethan went into the bathroom to dispose of the condom and do whatever men did after sex, Susan scrounged around for her underwear, then sifted through her purse for the big, baggy T-shirt she'd crammed beneath a year's supply of protection.

Okay, maybe not a year. But she'd hauled a lot of rubber with her. And on top of that, she'd just agreed to live with her brand-new lover. One afternoon of skyrocketing sex, and she was his for the taking.

Was that her method of not getting attached?

Disgusted with herself, she dragged her panties over her hips and pulled the T-shirt over her head. She would simply tell him that she'd made a mistake. That she couldn't possibly...

He came out of the bathroom, still naked, still looking tall and strong and erotic. The ultimate partner.

He sat on the edge of the bed, smiled at her comfy ensemble. "How cute you are. Warm and cozy. I'm glad you're going to stay here."

Her resolve shattered. She reached for him, felt the breadth of his shoulders, the comfort of bare skin. She'd always wanted to belong to him, and now she had her chance to play house, then let him go.

What could be more perfect than that?

"I'm glad, too." She skimmed his hair away from his forehead. It was in need of a trim, she noticed. Dark and tousled. "Are you hungry? I can make dinner."

"I'm starved. But there isn't much in my fridge." He lifted his jeans off the floor and zipped into them.

No boxers, she thought. He'd just climbed into his pants without underwear.

How sexy could one man be?

She sucked in a controlled breath. "I'm sure there's something I can fix."

"So you say. Wait until you look."

She was looking, and she liked what she saw. A solid chest, lean hips, the stomach she'd kissed.

He turned his head, distracted by a scratching sound. "My pesky mutts are at the door." He gave her a lopsided smile and leaped up. "I'm glad they didn't bug us earlier."

Susan went into the kitchen and tried to scrounge up some food. The contents in his refrigerator consisted of stale bread, a half-eaten block of cheddar cheese, a gallon of milk, too many condiments and a twelve-pack of beer.

"Do you live on ketchup and mustard?" she asked, when he came strolling in with three rambunctious dogs.

"I warned you."

She opened the freezer and found a jumbo-size bag of French fries and an even bigger container of ice cream. Amused by his sheepish grin, she checked the pantry. He was better off in the canned goods department if chili, chicken noodle soup and franks and beans counted as wholesome meals. The cereal they'd had for breakfast was in abundance, too. Oh, and canine food, lots of veterinarian-approved chow.

He waited, the dogs dancing at his feet. "What's the verdict?"

"Chili cheese fries and…" She poked around, found a can of peaches and held it up. "And these, with vanilla ice cream."

"Sounds good to me." He came up behind her and nuzzled her neck. "I've never lived with anyone before."

Her pulse fluttered. "Me, neither. This is probably going to take some getting used to." But even as she said it, she was turning in his arms, eager to kiss him, to cozy up with the man who'd just made delicious love to her.

Thirty minutes later they ate on the porch, devouring the messy French fry concoction from the same plate. By now they were both dressed. She'd wrapped a terry-cloth robe over her T-shirt and put on a pair of slippers. He'd opted for boots and a worn-out jacket, right along with his threadbare jeans.

Chocolate butted in, pestering for his fair share of the fries.

"Go away," Ethan told the dog. "You already ate."

"When has that ever stopped him?"

"Good point." He popped the top on his beer. "Why haven't you ever lived with anyone? I thought you were involved in some serious relationships."

"I was. They just never progressed to that level." She thought about the men she'd been committed to. "Keith was right after college, and Timothy came later."

"How much later?"

"A few years ago. He wanted me to be available for his schedule, his lifestyle." Corporate banking, she recalled. Boating on the weekends. "I tried to scale down, to give him more time, but I felt like I was cheating myself. My career."

"You're not working now," he pointed out.

"Because I came here to be with my family. It's the first extended stay I've ever had, aside from the year I lived here." She glanced up, sensed him watching her. "When I met you."

His face was shadowed, slightly hidden. "Is it tough, being away from your job?"

"I've been keeping in touch with my assistant, doing the best I can. But what's going on here is more pressing." She noticed the amulet around his neck, saw that it was catching a ray of moonlight, glinting against his shirt. "So much more."

He didn't say anything for a while. He just drank his beer and ate his food. Then he wiped his hands on his napkin and leaned forward to skim her robe, to touch her.

She knew that it was his way of comforting her, of letting her know he was thinking about Lily, too.

Chocolate barked and Susan gave the Lab a

French fry. He inhaled it, then sniffed around Ethan's beer.

"No way, pal," the vet said. "Go hang out with your buddies."

His buddies, Clark and Kent, were poised on the grass, snapping at insects that winged by.

The nocturnal hum made Susan sit back and listen. "It's peaceful here."

"It is. But this cabin's too small. I'll be glad when I can move into my own place. I wish we were there right now. I wish I could share it with you."

Warmed by his words, she wondered what his new house was like, what type of architectural features appealed to him. "You're my best friend, Ethan."

"You're mine, too." His teeth flashed in the dark. "Do you want to take a shower with me?"

Her pulse leaped. "When?"

He gestured to their meal. "As soon as the food's gone."

Susan noticed there were three whole fries and one glob of melted cheese left. "What about dessert?"

"We can do that after we soap each other down."

"Impatient, aren't you?"

"Yep." He stuffed the potatoes in his mouth. "Food's gone. Let's go."

She laughed and accepted his hand. He led her to the bathroom, where they stripped off their clothes and adjusted the water temperature.

"Can I wash your hair?" he asked. "With your shampoo?"

She agreed, and when they stepped into the cramped stall, he opened the bottle and inhaled the citrus scent. Fascinated, she watched him.

He looked up, moved closer, reached for her. "I like the way it smells."

And she liked the way he massaged her scalp with his strong, deft fingers, the suds dripping down her back.

She stepped under the showerhead, and he rinsed her hair, then added a smooth, creamy dollop of conditioner.

Afterward, she washed his hair, too. Then they kissed and caressed, making every warm, wet, soapy moment count. Water rained over their faces like a tropical mist.

He whispered something naughty in her ear, and she nearly climbed all over him.

The condom in his hand shimmered like a colorfully wrapped star. He turned it, spinning it between his fingers. She hadn't even seen him bring it into the shower.

"You're a magician," she said.

"You think so?" He opened the package, sheathed himself.

"Yes." She closed her eyes, and he pressed her against the wall, lifted her hips and joined his body with hers.

Making the rest of the world disappear.

Chapter 11

Susan pushed a shopping cart through the market, filling the basket with meat, eggs, fresh fruit and vegetables. She added several packages of pasta and the fixings for homemade marinara sauce, too.

She'd awakened this morning in Ethan's arms, feeling warm and intimate. And domestic, she reminded herself.

She liked living with Ethan.

She stopped in the coffee aisle and studied the brand he favored. It was the kind Lily and Ryan preferred, too. Suddenly she thought about her cousins, about how much the older couple loved each other.

Susan couldn't imagine being in love like that.

No, she thought. That wasn't true. Somewhere in the back of her mind she was already imagining it, already panicking about how easily it could happen.

Tempering the feeling, she grabbed a can of coffee, then tossed in her favorite blend of tea and a box of instant hot chocolate. Earlier, she'd gotten a ride to the main house to see Ryan, to tell him that she and Ethan were living together, but her cousin had been resting. From what Patrick had said, Ryan was in bad shape. Not only was he waiting desperately for Jason to contact him about Lily, he was battling symptoms of his tumor, as well.

Susan had left without seeing Ryan. She'd borrowed one of his vehicles, a truck with the Double Crown logo, and told the FBI she was headed to the market.

And here she was, shopping like a first-time bride.

When another customer stopped just a few feet away from her, Susan glanced at the other woman's cart. A toddler sat in the kiddie seat, his chubby little cheeks filled with the vanilla wafer he was eating. He flashed a slobbery grin, and her heart dropped to her stomach.

How many grandchildren did Ryan and Lily

have? Her brain was so scattered, she couldn't even remember.

She returned the boy's smile and darted on to another aisle, afraid she would cry in public, break down about brides and babies and a cousin who was falling apart without his wife.

By the time she returned to Ethan's cabin, her emotions were bent, like branches on a gnarled tree.

She put away the groceries and glanced at the kitchen clock. Ethan was at work, making his rounds. Susan wished she were working, too.

Refusing to remain idle, she called Sandy, her vivacious young assistant, and got an update about the hotline. They discussed the budget, the other employees, the ever-changing volunteers: details that had become second nature to Susan.

Finally she hung up the phone and wandered through the cabin, picking up after Ethan. He'd left his clothes from yesterday on the floor and his cereal bowl from this morning on an end table.

Next she tidied the bathroom, where he'd created another two-minute mess—a glob of toothpaste that had adhered itself to the counter, a loose cap that belonged to his mouthwash, damp towels in the corner.

She lifted the towels and dropped them into the hamper, feeling like a new bride again.

A moment later she made a face in the mirror. She had to stop thinking in terms of wedding vows.

Unable to back off, she tasted his toothpaste, then got strangely aroused, a lot like he did when he'd made use of her shampoo.

Before she got carried away, she went into the kitchen to fix a salad, using ingredients she'd bought. As she mixed olive oil and rice vinegar for the dressing, Chocolate nudged her knee, begging, as usual.

"You won't like this," she told him.

Refusing to take no for an answer, he barked at her.

"Fine. Here." She gave him a cherry tomato and the big, silly dog ate it, making a liar out of her.

The phone rang, sending her into the living room. She grabbed the portable receiver and heard Ethan's troubled voice.

"I screwed up, Susan."

"What do you mean? What's wrong?"

"I lost the amulet. When I left the cabin this morning I was wearing it, and now it's gone. It must have come loose and fallen off somewhere." He paused, cursed. "How could I be so stupid? I should have tightened the knot. I should have been more careful."

"Where are you?" she asked.

"Right now? I'm here at the Double Crown. But I've been all over today—other ranches, my clinic in town, the filling station. The amulet could be anywhere."

"Did you call those places? Check with the employees?"

"Yes, but I doubt they looked very hard. Other than my receptionist."

She sat on the edge of the couch. She hadn't been aware that he'd opened a clinic in town. Most mobile vets weren't set up to handle critical care, using referral centers instead. But now that she thought about it, his clinic made sense. Ethan was the ultimate caregiver.

"I'll help you search for the amulet," she said. "We'll start at the Double Crown and work our way back."

He breathed a grateful sigh into the phone. "Thanks. I'll come get you."

"I have wheels. I borrowed one of Ryan's trucks. Just tell me where to meet you and I'll be there as soon as I can."

"I'm at the foaling paddocks."

"Then that's where I'll be, too."

Within no time she was traveling along the ranch's inner roads, the pickup bumping and jarring on the way. She prayed that the necklace wasn't lost, that it was simply misplaced and waiting to be found.

Ethan was right where he said he would be, in the area that housed mares and foals. Although the

Double Crown was a cattle ranch, Ryan and Lily raised horses, too.

Susan moved closer to her lover, and they gazed at each other. She wanted to wrap her arms around him. He looked big and strong and much too worried.

"It's okay," she told him. "We won't quit until we find it."

"What if we don't? What if it's gone for good?" He touched the opening of his shirt, where the necklace had been. "Something bad could happen to Lily. Something even worse than what's already happened," he added, making chills run up and down Susan's spine.

"You stupid bitch." Jason's voice seethed in the dark, his words ringing in Lily's ear. "Did you think I wouldn't notice?"

She knew he was talking about the scrapes on her arms, the telltale sign that she'd been trying to cut the rope that bound her.

"I should kill you for that." He raised his tone a pitch. Then he kicked her in the ribs. Hard, so hard, she nearly choked beneath the gag.

Trembling, Lily fell to one side. She tried to escape in her mind, to slip into another place, another time, but the pain in her body reminded her of where she was.

Another sharp kick exploded, and she feared

that Jason would kill her. That he would pound her until there was nothing left to pound, until she lay, broken and bleeding and gasping for air.

"Say you're sorry." He intensified the pressure. "Kiss up to me."

Lily kept telling herself that she would rather die than succumb to Jason's demands. But that wasn't true. She didn't want to die. She wanted to go home to her husband, to her family. She wanted to be by Ryan's side when he slipped away, when heaven took him.

She heard Jason moving closer, kneeling on the ground next to her. In her mind, she told him to go to hell, to burn in a red-hot flame.

But behind the gag, she mumbled an apology.

Praying that he would spare her life.

Susan glanced at the ranch hands and foaling attendants she and Ethan had recruited in their search. Everyone was spread out, taking a different area. She sat in front of the first paddock, near the gate, sifting though leaves that had fallen from a nearby tree.

"What are you doing?"

She turned to the sound of Cathy's voice, meeting her gaze. She hadn't seen the rebellious teen since the first day they'd met. In the midst of the kidnapping chaos she'd lost track of the young girl she wanted to help.

"I'm looking for a necklace Ethan lost," Susan said.

"Then I'll bet this is it." Cathy reached into her pocket and produced the Apache charm.

"Oh, my God. Where did you find it?"

"Over there." The fourteen-year-old pointed to a metal shed, a location close to where Ethan's truck was parked. "It was under the door."

"Of his dually?"

"No. Of the building. I was in there—" Cathy paused, raised her chin, gave Susan a defiant look "—smoking. And that's when I noticed it."

Susan decided to ignore the teenager's smoking admission, at least for now. "Thank you so much. This is really important to Ethan." She took the amulet. "It was a gift from Lily."

Cathy's face went pale. "Do you think that guy killed her? Do you think she's dead?"

"No." Her heart twisted in her chest. "I believe she's coming home." She tightened her grip on the charm. "Soon."

"How can you be sure?"

"I can't. But I'm trying to think good thoughts. To do whatever I can to make a difference." Even trust in superstition, she thought. "Come on." She reached for Cathy's hand. "Let's tell Ethan that you found the necklace."

Cathy let herself be dragged along, for which

Susan was grateful. They approached Ethan, and when he saw the amulet, his breath rushed out.

"Cathy found it," Susan told him, explaining how the teenager had stumbled across the charm.

He smiled at the young girl, thanking her in earnest. Then he checked the leather cord and retied the knot that had come undone, making sure it was tight.

"I wonder if I should glue this," he said.

"That would probably be a good idea," Susan agreed. "I'm sure one of the ranch hands has some."

After Ethan secured a tube of epoxy and informed everyone that the necklace had been recovered, he invited Susan and Cathy to hang out while he finished his rounds.

Pleased, Susan gazed at her lover. Apparently he remembered that they were supposed to save Cathy. Or at least offer her an alternative to teenage mood swings and stolen cigarettes.

The girl shuffled her feet, digging her tennis shoes into the dirt. Just like last time, she wore jeans, a T-shirt and a messy ponytail.

"What are we supposed to do while you're working?" Cathy asked Ethan.

"You can visit with my favorite foal. She's being imprint trained. The friendliest little girl you'd ever want to meet."

She took step a closer. "Really?"

"Yep. Imprinting is a method that bonds horses to humans. It's a process that starts right after they're born."

He led Susan and Cathy into a paddock, introducing them to a pretty young filly and her mother. The foal came right up to them.

Cathy smiled. "What's her name?"

"Diamond's Gold Dust, but everyone calls her Dusty. Don't let her suck your fingers," he told the teenager as the foal nudged Cathy's hand. "That's not part of the training."

"Why not?"

"It leads to biting."

While Susan watched, he showed Cathy how to interact with Dusty. He let her know that the foal wasn't a pampered pet. The young horse was being taught to be submissive, responsive and obedient.

Susan bit back a smile. "Not like someone's dog we know."

Ethan arched his eyebrows. "Look who's talking. You give in to him, too."

Cathy shifted her stance. "You guys are talking about Chocolate, huh?"

"That's right." Ethan tugged on the teenager's ponytail. "And I've seen you slip him treats, too."

Although the young girl rolled her eyes, she seemed comfortable with his playful affection. Susan wasn't sure what Cathy thought of her.

"I better get busy," Ethan said, preparing to return to work. "I've got rounds to finish."

Within no time, he said goodbye and closed the gate behind him, leaving Susan and Cathy alone.

They stood in silence for a while, with a slight breeze rustling the air. Then Susan broke the ice. "I heard your mom is pregnant. That you're going to have a baby brother or sister."

Cathy looked up, where she'd been enjoying the foal's attention. A frown furrowed her brow. "So?"

Susan held her gaze. "I think it's nice that your parents are going to have another child."

"Yeah, well, I think it's dumb."

"You do?" She cocked her head. "Why?"

"I don't know." The teenager remained close to the mare and her offspring. "It just seems like a hassle."

Susan didn't respond. Instead she watched the way Cathy had endeared herself to horse and baby.

"I think you'll make a great sister," she finally said.

Cathy didn't budge. "How would you know?"

"Because I can tell that you care."

The teenager chewed on a strand of her hair, a tendril that had come loose from her ponytail. "My parents are bugging me to be there when the baby's born. Right in the delivery room."

"They just want you to accept what's happening. To be part of it." She shifted her gaze and saw that Dusty was nursing, drinking her mother's milk. "This is a monumental event in your lives."

Cathy scrunched up her face, making the freckles on her nose disappear. "Have you ever seen a baby being born?"

"Not a human baby, but I saw a foal being delivered. It was a long time ago, though, when I lived here during high school."

"Was it gross?"

"No. It was really sweet." Susan remembered how captivated she'd been. "Do you want me to ask Ethan if you can attend a foaling when the next mare goes into labor?" She turned in the direction of the pasture, where a group of pregnant mares grazed. "There seems to be enough of them."

"I guess. As long as it's not gross."

Susan smiled. "It isn't. I swear."

Cathy managed a small smile, too. Then, without warning, she decided it was time to take off, to do her homework. Susan suspected that the young girl didn't want to talk anymore, to reveal too much of herself.

But Ethan used to be abrupt when he was young, too. He would only let a conversation take him so far. In actuality, Cathy had offered more information about her family than Ethan ever had.

Susan wasn't sure what that meant.

A moment later she caught sight of him in another paddock. He looked so familiar, so right in the equine setting. He was dressed in varying shades of denim, with his favorite straw hat seated low on his head.

And even though she couldn't see the amulet around his neck, she knew it was there.

Creating hope.

Jason removed the gag, practically ripping the fabric from Lily's mouth.

"Say it," he said. "Say it out loud."

Her voice cracked. "I'm sorry."

"Again," he snarled. "But with more feeling."

"I'm sorry." She swallowed her pride, telling herself this was the only way to survive, to see her family again. "I'll be good from now on."

"Damn right you will." He sounded giddy with power, on the verge of demonic euphoria. "Have you figured out yet where you are?"

She shook her head.

"Do you want to see?"

She nodded, praying this wasn't a trick. A way to get her to look into his eyes while he beat her or raped her or tortured her to death.

"Then get ready. Here we go."

He tore off the blindfold, and the first thing she saw was his face, illuminated by a small lantern. She blinked and tried to adjust her sight, to take in her surroundings, where a bigger lantern exposed walls and floors.

She was in a cave, with ominous shapes twisting and turning. She knew the formations were beautiful, but in her situation, they seemed haunted and ghostlike.

The leaky faucet she'd imagined didn't exist. The beads of water echoing in the distance were a natural part of the environment, probably forming tiny crystals on the walls.

"It's dark down here all the time," Jason said. "A place where no one will find you. This cave isn't open to the public anymore. Portions of it collapsed a long time ago."

"You carried me down here?"

"Yes, and it was quite an effort." He turned his head, showcasing his profile, the hard angles and cruel lines. "This is almost over."

"It is?"

"Yes. After I get the money, I'll reveal your whereabouts." He sat back on his haunches. He was in his thirties, strong and agile. "I have a brilliant escape plan." He leaned in close. "But your rescue might be a bit of a problem. You might even die."

No, she thought. She wanted to live. To laugh. To love. To watch her grandchildren grow.

"When?" she asked. "When is this going to happen?"

"Tomorrow. As soon as Ryan receives my next tape." He put the gag back into place, then covered her eyes, shutting out the golden beams of light.

And leaving her in the dark once again.

Chapter 12

Morning erupted in a blast of energy. Ethan did
his damnedest to keep track of everything that
was going on around him. Per Patrick's request, he
and Susan had gone to the main house. And now
they were sweating bullets.

A message had arrived from Jason, giving Ryan
cryptic instructions. He was supposed to drive to
the Saddle Tramp Motel in the Hill Country, check
into a room and wait for further contact.

No cops, no FBI. Except for Emmett Jamison.

Jason was allowing his special agent brother to
get involved, to accompany Ryan on the drop.

As for the rest of the team, they were being dispatched in a covert operation, where they would remain in the background, undetected by the kidnapper.

Or at the least that was the plan.

Ethan wasn't familiar with the inner workings of the FBI, but he recognized organized chaos when he saw it. Each and every agent knew his place, his job.

"This is torture," Patrick said.

"I know." Ethan glanced at Susan. She was watching Ryan. He was being fitted with a bulletproof vest and a wire that would keep him connected to the group.

Patrick spoke again. "They offered to replace Ryan with a lookalike, but he refused."

"Can you blame him?" Ethan asked. "If it were my wife, I'd do exactly what he's doing."

"Me, too. But he just looks so damn frail."

That was true. Ryan was gaunt, the shadows under his eyes dogging his rugged features. His illness hovered like an open flame, singeing his strength.

"He's going to do just fine." This came from Susan, who twisted her hands on her lap.

"Of course he is." Ethan sat next to her on the sofa and stilled her jittery fingers. She turned to look at him, and he felt the weight of her gaze. The depth, the emotion, the connection only lovers could share.

For one stolen moment, for one instant in time, they got lost in the safety net they'd created.

In each other, he thought.

Then reality returned. Voices, footsteps, electronic devices, the lingering aroma of leftover coffee.

Susan took an audible breath, making Ethan want to hold her. He could see that she was struggling to bury her fears.

She came to her feet and approached Ryan. He reached for her and she embraced him, letting him know that she loved him. That no matter what, she would be waiting.

For him. For Lily. For both of them to come home.

The Saddle Tramp was located in a Hill Country town that boasted German roots. But to Ryan, it looked like a typical Texas motel with wood trim and wagon-wheel accents.

With his pulse pounding in his throat, he glanced at Emmett, who sat next to him, manning the SUV. The agent cut the engine and surveyed the parking lot. Ryan wasn't sure what the other man was looking for. But he was glad that Emmett Jamison was on his side.

The rest of the FBI, the team that was trailing them, was nowhere to be seen. But Ryan knew they were out there somewhere, ready to take orders, to close in if the situation demanded it.

"Let's go," Emmett said.

Ryan nodded, wishing his stomach wasn't cramping, jumping in nervous spasms. Was Lily here? Was she hurt? Drugged? Alive? Dead?

"Keep it together," the agent told him.

"I am." He walked toward the front desk. Beside him, Emmett seemed cool and calm. No outward signs of adrenaline. No indication that their luggage consisted of a two-million-dollar ransom.

They rented a room and waited, just as they'd been instructed to do. And within no time, a bouquet of lilies arrived at their door.

Lily. Lilies. Ryan almost wept.

Emmett tipped the delivery person, closed the door, then opened the card, reading it out loud. "Canyon Caverns at one o'clock. Don't be late."

The agent glanced at his watch and cursed.

Ryan checked the time, too. Canyon Caverns was a group of caves deep in the hills. They had to get on the road as quickly as possible or they'd never make it by one.

On the way Emmett contacted the other agents. He told them that they needed to find an experienced caver, someone who knew the area. And they needed equipment for everyone on the team—lights, ropes, harnesses, pulleys, helmets, cable ladders, underwater gear.

"Just in case," he said to Ryan.

"I understand." Although his stomach was still cramping, Ryan trusted Emmett Jamison. Especially now, while they were chasing shadows, following Jason's every move. Emmett, of all people, should be able to delve into Jason's mind.

To predict what came next.

The inner courtyard smelled of herbs and flowers and mint-flavored tea. Susan sat in the swing, surrounded by a vine-covered arbor, steam rising from the cup in her hand.

Rosita was in the kitchen, preparing lunch, making food for people who would only pretend to eat. The housekeeper didn't live with Ryan and Lily. She and her husband had their own home on the Double Crown.

Ethan came outside, and Susan said the first words that came to mind, "If Rosita and Ruben lived here, do you think Jason would have gotten away with kidnapping Lily?"

He frowned and sat next to her, rocking the ancient swing, making the hinges creak. "Don't do this to yourself."

"But if there were more people sleeping here that night. If someone—"

He touched his finger to her lips, silencing her.

In the background a fountain bubbled, like a well without wishes. No shiny coins. No dreams.

"It's over," he said. "There's no such thing as going back in time."

She snared his gaze. "We did it."

"Who? You and me?" He spoke softly, slowly, the way he used to when they were young. A slight drawl. A boyish slant. "Are you sure about that?"

"Yes."

"No, we didn't." He took her tea and set it on the ground. The delicate saucer rattled. "We started over. We started fresh."

She looked at him. Really looked at him. Close enough to see every pore, every whisker he'd neglected to shave that morning. There was so much she didn't know about him, so much she still had to learn. "Sometimes it feels the same. You're so elusive, Ethan. So hard to grasp."

He put his hand on her knee. "That's the sadness talking. The fear. The worry."

Was it? At this point, she couldn't be sure. Memories were tumbling in her mind, making her homesick for Lily and Ryan, for seeing them together. "I'm so scared for them."

"I know. But it will be over soon. The FBI will bring Lily home."

"And what about Jason?" she asked. "Are they going to catch him?"

"They have to," he told her. "It can't end any other way."

Silent, she looked at Ethan again. Strands of hair fell across his eyebrows, jagged yet straight, like marks of lightning. "When this is over, will you make love with me?"

He slid his fingers through hers. "You know I will."

"Outside? In the wind? In the rain?"

He glanced up, but the sky wasn't visible, not through the arbor. "Is it supposed to rain tonight?"

She nodded, filling her lungs with air. She knew her emotions were out of sync. That this was an inopportune time to crave him, to seek passion, to let her heart run away with her.

But somewhere deep down she thought Ryan and Lily would approve. That they would understand.

At precisely one o'clock, Ryan spotted Lily's truck parked on the side of the narrow road that led to Canyon Caverns. The license plate was different, the custom wheels were gone, and there were deliberate dents that made the vehicle look old and beat-up. But Ryan knew it was his wife's brand-new Dodge.

"Jason must have another mode of transportation now," Emmett said. "Probably a stolen motorcycle that he hauled to this location in Lily's truck." He looked out the windshield, at the hilly terrain. "The bike is probably hidden in the brush somewhere."

Ryan's pulse jumped. "Maybe Lily is in the Dodge."

Emmett shook his head. "He's not going to turn her over to us until he gets the money." He parked behind the truck. "This is where he left our next instructions."

"I have a key. I always keep an extra set on me." Ryan fumbled, digging his keys out of his pocket and dropping them in the process. His hands were trembling.

The agent touched his shoulder, giving it a light squeeze, offering silent support.

They searched the Dodge from top to bottom and found the instructions, along with a portable GPS, a global positioning system.

Emmett read the handwritten note. "Follow the coordinates programmed in the GPS. It will take you to the opening of the Crystal Night cave. Be there at one-twenty. Bring the money."

While Ryan and Emmett drove farther up the mountain, using the GPS, the agent contacted his team.

Ryan listened to the preparations the FBI was making. The equipment was on its way, and a park ranger who was a member of a national cave rescue association was being escorted to the site.

He knew the layout of Canyon Caverns and could familiarize the team with the terrain.

When Ryan and Emmett came to a stretch of land that was no longer accessible by car, they continued on foot, using the GPS and carrying duffel bags filled with cash. Ryan knew he was a hindrance. A tired, sick old man trying to keep up. But he refused to stop, to rest. They only had five minutes to reach the opening of the Crystal Night cave.

Susan, Ethan and Patrick ate lunch in the dining room, with Rosita clucking around them like a nervous hen, trying to comfort them with food, with the only help she knew how to give.

Susan tasted the roast, forcing herself to take a bite. Ethan sat next to her, and when their gazes locked, her heartbeat tumbled. He was there for her, right there—her friend, her protector, her lover.

The man Ryan thought she was going marry.

She studied the rosebud pattern on her plate, the tiny flowers and gold-tipped leaves. She could almost imagine walking down the aisle with him. Yet she knew it was a crazy thought. Unrealistic. Dreamy. Dangerous.

Patrick gazed out the window. "It's getting cloudy out there."

Ethan caught Susan's gaze again, repeating what she'd told him earlier. "It's supposed to rain."

The older man continued to look out the window. "When?"

"Tonight," Ethan responded.

"I wish I could have gone with them." Patrick paused, picked up his butter knife, gripping the silver handle so hard, his knuckles turned white. "I can't stand waiting around. Sitting here. Doing nothing."

"Neither can I." Susan found her voice, shaky as it was. "But we don't have a choice."

Ethan broke eye contact and reached for his water. Susan's thoughts drifted to Ryan and Lily, to the difficulties they'd endured. The decades they'd spent apart. The lost years. The other marriages.

She stole a glance at her lover and saw that he'd barely touched his food. He noticed her watching him, then reached for her hand.

Susan held tight. Too tight, she thought.

Anxious, she released a choppy breath. Was she falling in love? Tripping over her heart? Over the ache in her chest?

Yes, she thought. She was.

She loved Ethan Eldridge, a man she was sure to lose.

And now, more than ever, she wanted Ryan

to find his wife, to be with her for as long as he could.

No matter what the odds.

The opening of the cave was a narrow hole that led to a pitch-black drop in what looked like the center of the earth.

Emmett couldn't see Jason. He couldn't see a damn thing. But he knew his brother was down there.

He turned to look at Ryan. The older man stood back, away from the opening, from the danger of falling. Emmett could tell that Ryan was dizzy, overexerted from their short hike.

"This is it," Emmett said.

Ryan nodded, then cleared his throat, waiting, it seemed, for what came next.

Emmett remained a safe distance from the opening, too. Then he took a step forward, just one step and called his brother's name.

"Jason!" His voice echoed in the chamber. "It's me."

"Is Ryan with you?" a voice echoed back, as if it were coming from the depths of hell.

Emmett glanced at his companion. "Yes."

"Who else is out there?" his brother wanted to know.

"No one."

"Liar," Jason challenged. "I'll bet you've got

other agents with you. Hiding like the federal slugs they are. But it doesn't matter. They won't catch me."

Yes, they will, Emmett thought. As soon as the caving equipment arrived, they would beat Jason at his own game.

Ryan yelled into the hole, his words straining with the effort. "We brought what you asked for. We followed your instructions. Now let me talk to my wife."

"Not yet. Make the drop first."

"Just let the bags go?" Emmett asked.

"Drop them into the cave. One at a time."

Emmett couldn't gauge the exact distance. He couldn't tell how far it was. But Jason knew. His brother had probably tested the results of a similar plunge.

He did as he was told, then waited for a response. In the silence he stepped back and contacted the team, letting them know what was happening, keeping them informed.

A small light flashed from the cave, and he realized Jason was scanning the contents of the duffel bags, checking to see if they were filled with cash, making sure there were no tracking devices attached.

"We did our part," Emmett called out. "Now let us talk to Lily."

"She isn't here," came the echoed reply. "She's in another cave."

"Which one? Give us the GPS coordinates."

"No way! She's my ticket out of here. I strapped a bomb to her. It's not powerful enough to take down the whole mountain, but it will destroy the cave she's in, killing her and anyone else who's near it."

Emmett glanced at Ryan. The old man's face had gone pale, as white as a ghost on Halloween.

He turned away from the panicked husband, gazing into the black pit instead. "What are your demands?" he asked his brother. "Tell us how to save the hostage."

"You can start by searching for her. In every cave but this one. You can use all that manpower you brought to find her and leave me alone." A pause, then, "The explosives are on a timer. You've got forty minutes before it goes off, but I can detonate the charge from here, too."

Ryan swayed on his feet, giving Emmett a pleading look.

Jason continued, "And don't even think about bringing in helicopters. If I hear a chopper, I'll flip the switch." He made a menacing sound. "If anyone tries to follow me, it's over. Lily Fortune is dead."

Lily sat in the dark, bound, blindfolded and gagged. Jason had bragged about the bomb, insisting how clever he was, reciting things that had fogged her mind.

She didn't know anything about primers, timers, chemical compounds or the velocity of detonation. Rogue science was something men like Jason probably uncovered on the Internet.

But to her, it meant destruction.

When silence threatened to swallow her, she listened to the tortured cadence of her own heart.

Then she thought about Ryan, about the man she loved.

Was he nearby? Did he know that she was trapped with an explosive device attached to her back?

Afraid to move, afraid the charge would erupt, she sat rock still. How much time had passed? How long had she been waiting? Wondering if she would survive?

Suddenly a montage of memories sluiced through her brain, like a jumbled movie playing in her head.

People, places, choppy images.

The cliché of death, she thought. Her life flashing before her eyes.

Lily willed away the images and focused on being rescued instead. On a big strong angel sweeping her into his arms and carrying her into the light.

* * *

Ryan couldn't think straight. Everything was spinning in circles, turning at a dizzying pace. The equipment had just arrived and now the FBI agents were separating into different teams, preparing for the rescue.

According to the park ranger, there were four caves where Lily could be. Two were wild, left in their natural state with no man-made improvements. And the other two were show caves that had sustained damage over the years and were no longer available for public tours.

Although a bomb squad had been notified, they might not arrive in time. But as far as Ryan could tell, some of the agents who were already in attendance were demolition experts. That gave him hope.

Heart-thundering hope.

He glanced at Emmett, who was gearing up to enter one of the show caves. The other men on his team were preparing, as well.

Ryan knew the FBI wasn't going to allow him to get involved. He didn't have any search-and-rescue training. And on top of that, he was too ill to rappel into holes, to cross dilapidated bridges or crawl through narrow passages. He couldn't swim in underground lakes or drag his feet through ankle-deep mud.

Ryan couldn't look for his wife; he couldn't do

a damn thing but wait. Soon he would be moved to a different location. He would still be in the area, just out of harm's way.

Emmett turned to face him. "Jason could be bluffing," he said. "The bomb could be a scare tactic, a trick to buy more time. But there's no way to be sure. Not at this point."

Ryan met the agent's determined gaze. Either way, the FBI was taking the threat seriously. Four caves. Four rescue teams. They had less than an hour to create a miracle.

To find Lily.

Then capture the bastard who'd kidnapped her.

Chapter 13

Ryan waited, his heart pounding with every second, every minute, every fear-steeped passage of time.

He was on a road that provided a long-distance view of Canyon Caverns. By now there were ambulances standing by, emergency vehicles that had arrived with their red lights flashing.

He glanced at the special agent standing next to him. The other man wasn't a member of the original unit. He'd showed up later. But he was still a vital part of the operation. He was communicating with the rescue teams.

He appeared strong and steady, more than capable of holding down the fort. Unlike Ryan, who was ready to fall apart.

What if the whole thing was a lie, a game Jason was playing? What if Lily was already dead?

Suddenly he saw a trio of white vans traveling toward the caves.

"It's the bomb squad," the agent told him. "They're a type-one team," he added. "They handle complex incidents."

Ryan knew that was supposed to make him feel better, but it didn't. They were running on borrowed time.

And Lily's life was at stake.

A moment later the agent got his attention. "They found her!"

"What?"

"Your wife. I just got radio confirmation. They found her. She's safe."

Ryan nearly sank to the ground. The bomb squad vehicles were still headed up the hill. They were late, but it didn't matter.

Lily was alive.

"The device that was attached to her was a dummy," the agent said. "No active charge." He gestured to the moving vans. "But now that they're here, they'll do a complete sweep."

Ryan took a deep breath. "Is Lily out of the cave? Did they get her out of there?"

The other man nodded. "It was Agent Jamison's team who carried out the rescue."

Emmett, Ryan thought. Jason's brother had saved her.

Emmett entered Lily Fortune's hospital room, keeping his footsteps soft and quiet. Night had long since fallen, and he noticed everyone in the room was asleep.

Everyone but Ethan Eldridge.

They exchanged a silent nod, and Emmett moved closer to the bed. Lily looked fragile, with her eyes closed and an IV drip in her arm. Her husband dozed beside her, on top of the blanket, where he held her hand.

Emmett tried to relax, but his stomach was tied up in knots. Jason had gotten away. His brother had escaped, killing a federal agent in the process. A massive manhunt was still underway, but that did little to ease the tension in Emmett's gut. Jason was his responsibility. The criminal he'd vowed to catch.

He glanced at Ethan again. The veterinarian sat next to Susan Fortune, and although both of them occupied stiff, utilitarian chairs, they'd found a way to stay close. She'd nodded off with her head against his shoulder, and he rested a protective arm around her.

"Did you see Patrick in the hall?" Ethan asked in a slightly hushed tone.

Emmett responded in the same low-pitched voice. "We spoke for a few minutes. He was with some other family members."

Ethan nodded, then studied the patient. "Lily thinks you're her angel."

Uncomfortable, Emmett moved away from the bed. Lily had called him some such thing when he'd found her, bound and gagged in the cave. "The bomb was a fake. Jason was bluffing. He even made Lily believe it was true."

"I know, but you were prepared to face an explosion. To risk your life to save hers."

"That's part of my job."

"Is it?" The other man angled his head. "I think it's more to you than that. What you did for Lily and Ryan was heroic."

Heroic? An agent had died and his brother had disappeared with the ransom. "I don't need you talking me up."

Ethan squinted at him, and they exchanged a steely stare. Two men in a darkened hospital room. It seemed absurd, but Emmett couldn't deal with unwarranted praise. On the other hand, Ethan appeared to be a decent guy, someone who gave a damn. He didn't deserve Emmett's guilt-ridden wrath.

"I'm going to catch Jason," Emmett said. "I won't quit until I find him."

"I figured as much." When Susan stirred in her sleep, Ethan held her a little tighter. "But what about Ryan and Lily's safety? Can the FBI help with that?"

"I'll make sure that they continue to receive federal protection. That we keep agents stationed at the ranch." He glanced at the bed. "But I doubt that Ryan is going to let Lily out of his sight. Or that she'll let him out of hers."

"He doesn't have long to live."

Emmett blew out a rough breath. "I know."

Ethan shifted his gaze to Ryan. "I wonder if the hospital will let him stay with his wife tonight."

"I imagine they will." Lily was being treated for dehydration, mild abrasions and bruised ribs. But Ryan Fortune was terminally ill. "It seems only right."

"Yes, it does." Ethan turned his head and brushed his lips against Susan's hair. A natural reflex. Something he probably wasn't even aware of.

Emmett fell silent, then decided it was time to go back to work, to stop being drawn to other people's lives.

Focusing on his job, he said goodbye and exited the room, leaving behind both sets of lovers, old and young.

* * *

As Ethan drove to the cabin, he looked over at Susan, thinking how beautiful she was.

She smoothed her hair and gave him a small smile. "I can't believe I fell asleep at the hospital."

"It's okay. You've been running on empty."

"I'm so glad Lily is safe." She shifted in her seat, her voice turning raw. From emotion. From a long, heart-wrenching day. "But it didn't end the way it was supposed to."

He knew she was referring to Jason's escape and the federal agent he'd killed. "The FBI will catch him."

"When?" She sighed and glanced out the window, fogging the glass.

"I don't know." He thought about Emmett Jamison, about how determined the other man seemed. He wanted to believe that Emmett would apprehend his brother, but there were no guarantees.

"Jason has two million in cash." She frowned into the night, where the road curved and trees loomed. "He'll probably leave the country."

Ethan didn't say anything. He had no idea what Jason would do. But at least the FBI was taking precautions. They weren't leaving anything to chance.

By the time they reached the cabin, he and Susan had turned quiet. He parked his truck, and they left the vehicle and walked up the porch steps. When they entered the cabin, the dogs greeted them in a cozy welcome.

"It feels good to be home," she said.

Home. The word hit Ethan like a jagged-edged rock. The hunting cabin wasn't their home. He wouldn't be living here for much longer and neither would Susan.

She took a few minutes to change and remove her makeup. He liked how she looked with her face scrubbed clean and a nightgown flowing around her ankles.

Ethan stayed in his jeans. He didn't feel like getting ready for bed. He needed a bit more time to unwind.

After feeding the dogs, he rummaged through the pantry and located the hot chocolate Susan had bought. He held up the box. "Do you want some?"

She leaned against the counter, looking soft and ethereal, with her delicate garment and ladylike slippers. "That sounds good."

He heated the water in a pan, his heart constricting his chest. He didn't want to lose Susan. He didn't want her to return to California. But he knew she belonged in San Francisco. That she was, and always would be, a city girl.

Like his mom.

"Are you all right?" she asked.

He realized he was frowning, making too much

of their relationship, of an attachment he didn't want to feel, of the anguish his father had faced. "I'm fine." He opened the hot chocolate packets, dumped them into mismatched cups and added water that had begun to boil. "Did you buy marshmallows?"

"No, but they're already in there. The little freeze-dried kind."

"Oh." He glanced at the mixture he was stirring and saw that she was right. "Then we're all set." He handed her a mug of the warm brew.

She blew on the rim of the cup and looked directly into his eyes. "It's starting to rain."

He listened for the sound of water falling from the sky and heard intermittent drops touching the roof. Lightly, he thought, ever so lightly. "So it is."

She moved closer. "You promised to make love with me." She glanced at the window. "Out there."

His pulse shimmied, right down to his groin, electrifying his zipper, making his breath catch. "You'll get cold. You'll get wet."

"I'll wear a jacket. And boots."

He couldn't help but smile. "With your nightgown?"

She nodded, then kissed him. He decided she was the most erotic creature on earth. Every cell in his body begged for relief, for rain-dampened sex, for the crazy impulse that was making him hot and hard.

They stumbled to the armoire so she could put on a knee-length coat and replace her slippers with Western boots. He grabbed a condom, fisting the packet in his hand.

Once they were outside, they stood on the porch and scanned the yard, where trees, grass and shrubs glistened with water.

She took his hand and led him to a big gothic oak. They stood beneath it, leaves flurrying above their heads.

Enthralled, he touched her cheek. Rain sprinkled her face and created shimmering beads in her hair. A full moon dusted the darkness, and the air felt cool and crisp and strangely romantic.

Her coat was unbuttoned, revealing the front of her nightgown. The water-spotted material clung to her skin, outlining her breasts and the hardened peaks of her nipples.

When she removed her panties and tucked them into her pocket, he kissed her, tasting chocolate and marshmallows and the sweet sin they were about to commit.

Lust. Heartache. Emotional warfare.

She unzipped his jeans and pushed her hand inside, making him shiver. He kept his eyes open. He didn't dare blink. He didn't want to lose sight of her.

She stroked him, from shaft to tip. And then she dropped to the ground, right there on the wet grass, and gave him the most incredible oral sex he'd ever had.

Beautiful torture.

He tangled his hands in her hair. And when he couldn't stand it any longer, he switched places with her, falling to his knees and lifting the hem of her nightgown, doing to her what she'd done to him.

He licked her soft and slow, and she came against his tongue, arching her hips, telling him that she wanted more.

That she wanted him inside her.

Ethan feared he would lose his mind. He rose to his feet and fumbled with the condom. Anxious, he pressed her against the tree, and she adjusted her body to accept his penetration, to take him hard and deep.

He moved inside her, the sensation warm and slick. She clung to him, making throaty little sounds. When she gasped, he thrust deeper, then covered her mouth with his.

As they kissed, the wind howled, escaping into the night. She tore open the front of his shirt, but he didn't care. He craved her touch, the raw, wicked bite of her nails, the way she clawed his skin.

And at that desperate moment, he understood her passion, her need, the reason she wanted to make love in the rain.

To create a heart-hammering image, a memory neither of them would ever forget.

Susan stood at the window in Ethan's kitchen, gazing at the land, at the ranch her family owned. Four days had passed since the night of the kidnapping rescue. Lily was home from the hospital and settling quietly back into her life. Susan had spent time with her, helping her heal, helping her shed the emotional scars. The rest of the family was rallying around Lily, too, offering her the love and support she needed.

"Hey, gorgeous." Ethan's voice sounded behind her.

She turned around. He was dressed for work, with a denim shirt tucked into a pair of old Wrangler jeans. His hair was damp from the shower and combed away from his face. He still hadn't gotten it trimmed.

"Hey, yourself." She touched his freshly shaven jaw. She hadn't told him that she loved him. She hadn't found the courage to say it out loud. "Do you have time for breakfast?"

He shook his head. "No. But you can fix me dinner tonight."

"I can, huh?" She tugged him closer for a kiss, not wanting to think about the future, about the reality of leaving him.

He deepened the kiss, and she held on to him.

He tasted like citrus-flavored toothpaste, like oranges on a winter day.

When they separated, he smiled. "I have a gift for you." He pressed something into her hand, closing her fingers around it.

She opened her palm and saw a heart-shaped pendant necklace. White gold with tiny diamonds. Stunned, she looked up at him.

"It's Valentine's Day," he said.

"It…is?" She stumbled over her words. She'd lost track of time, of the date on the calendar.

He nodded, then crammed his hands into his pockets, keeping them there, looking a bit shy. "It came in one of those velvet boxes but I didn't want to wrap it and all that. I didn't want to make a big deal out of it."

But it was a big deal, she thought. Her eyes turned watery, filling with tears. She wanted to cry in his arms, but she summoned the strength to smile, to keep herself from breaking down. "It's beautiful." The kind of gift a man bought for the woman he loved. "Thank you, Ethan."

"You're welcome."

"Will you help me put it on?"

"Of course I will."

When he moved her hair out of the way, her knees went weak. Was he falling in love with her? Was he struggling with his feelings? The way she battled hers?

She touched the pendant, tracing the shape of the heart. The diamonds shimmered against her skin.

"I better go," he said.

Susan met his gaze. "This means a lot to me."

"It's just something I wanted you to have." He brushed his lips against her cheek, then stepped back and grabbed his hat, slipping it on his head, shielding his eyes. "I'll see you later."

She walked onto the porch and watched him leave. After she returned to the cabin, she removed some steaks from the freezer, thawing them out for dinner, for the meal she would prepare when he got home.

Should she buy him a gift, too? Give him something as personal as he gave her? At times Ethan still confused her.

Ten minutes later a knock sounded at the door, making Chocolate scamper around her feet. "Who's here?" she asked the dog as he perked his ears.

Susan answered the summons and found Cathy on the other side, dressed for school and carrying a tin of Valentine cookies.

More hearts, she thought. More emotion.

"These are from my mom." Cathy pushed the cookies toward her. "She would have brought them herself but she's babysitting today." The teenager motioned to a truck with its engine running. "That's my dad."

Susan waved to the gray-haired man behind the wheel, and he waved back. "Is he taking you to the bus stop?"

"Yes, but only because we had to come here first. This cabin is in the boonies, too far for me to walk." She shifted her feet. "It's kind of early, but my dad has to go to work."

"If you want to stay for a little while, I'll drive you."

"I'll have to ask my dad." Cathy ran to the truck and returned. "He said it's okay. My parents heard you were a psychologist. That you work with kids my age. They even looked up information about your hotline on the Internet." She blew her bangs out of her eyes. "I guess they think I'll get some free therapy out of this."

Susan clutched the cookies and smiled. "I don't mind."

Cathy shrugged. "I guess I don't, either. The hotline you run sounds pretty cool."

"Thank you." She thought about her job, the career that would take her back to California, separating her from Ethan. "It's very important to me." And so, God help her, was the man she'd fallen in love with.

Then stay with him, she told herself. Relocate to Texas. Her career shouldn't be a stumbling

block. She could run a national hotline from anywhere. She could—

"Are you okay?"

Susan blinked, then looked at Cathy. "I just
have a few things on my mind. But I'll be fine."
She searched the young girl's gaze, realizing she
was anxious to talk. "And so will you."

They went into the cabin, where they sat in
the living room, drinking milk and sampling the
candy-sprinkled treats.

Cathy dropped some crumbs onto her lap. "My
parents found out."

"That you smoke?"

"Yes." The girl frowned. "They gave me a bro-
chure about lung cancer."

"Your health is important. It should be the main
issue." Susan flashed back to her own youth, to
the rebellion that drove her. "I smoked when I was
your age, too."

"Is that why you never ragged on me about it?"

"I was waiting for the right time to talk to
you about it. If I ragged on you right away, you
wouldn't have liked me very much." She waited a
beat. "Are you going to quit?"

"I don't know. Maybe." Cathy blew out a heavy
sigh. "Is Lily okay now?"

"Yes. She's doing fine."

"And what about Ryan? Is he going to die from
his brain tumor?"

A concerned question, Susan thought. That deserved an honest answer. "Yes, he is. It's a terminal condition."

"My dad's the same age as Ryan."

"Is your father ill?"

"No."

"Are you afraid he might get sick?"

"Sometimes."

"Have you talked to him about this? Or to your mom?"

"No."

"You should." Susan closed the cover on the cookies, keeping them away from Chocolate. "You should tell them how you feel."

"I told them about what you said. About how I could be there when a foal is born. They thought that was good. That it might get me ready for the baby."

"I think so, too." She looked into Cathy's eyes, but the teenager glanced away. "Do you still think it's dumb that your parents are having another child?"

"It will be if my dad gets sick and me and my mom and the baby have to live on our own."

Susan shook her head. "That's not likely to happen."

"It could."

"Yes, but why worry about it? Why put those ideas in your head? Your father is older than most dads, but he's healthy. Strong enough to father another child. To be concerned about you and your smoking."

"I guess." Cathy dropped another crumb. "But I wish he wouldn't have moved us to Texas. Most of the kids at my school are weird. All the girls with their big hair, and the boys with their shit-kicker boots."

"Now you're going to make me laugh."

"Well, it's true."

A moment later they both laughed. Silly, girlish laughter that felt incredibly good.

"Texans are a bit strange," Susan said. "But I swear, they grow on you."

"Like Ethan's growing on you?"

"Yes," she said, touching her new necklace, clutching the heart, holding on to it. "Just like that."

Chapter 14

Susan created a romantic ambience, using items she'd borrowed from Lily. She placed a white candle in the center of the table and added a small vase of wildflowers. Stoneware china and linen napkins came next.

The gift she'd purchased, wrapped in Valentine paper and topped with a red bow, went beside Ethan's plate.

Anxious, she scattered a few more candles around the room, lighting each one and watching them flicker.

Finally she went into the kitchen and put the finishing touches on a festive salad, adding garlic-seasoned croutons. She decided to wait to mix the dressing since she didn't know if Ethan liked oil and vinegar.

After dusting crouton crumbs from her finger, she checked on the rest of the meal. The potatoes were baking in the oven and the steaks were marinating in a honey and pineapple glaze. Once Ethan got home, she would broil them.

Fifteen minutes later he arrived, looking slightly rumpled from a day's work. He sent her a warm smile, and her heart all but melted.

When he gave her a husbandly type kiss, she struggled with her composure.

He removed his hat and glanced around. "You've got this place all jazzed up. Hey, look at the table." He walked over to his place setting and picked up the gift. "Is this for me?"

Susan nodded. Her mind was going a mile a minute, caught in the bride mode.

"Can I open it?" he asked.

"I'm sorry. What?"

"My present. Can I open it?"

He looked like a kid at Christmas. A big, sexy kid with rugged features and a five-o'clock shadow.

"Yes, of course," she said.

He pulled off the bow and went after the paper. When he got to the box, he was a bit more careful. He opened it and examined his gift—a pocketknife with a shimmering blade and a decorative handle.

"Thank you. This is perfect. How did you know that I collect pocketknives?"

"I didn't. I knew that you always carried one, but it was Ryan who told me that you collected them. I had no idea what to get you, so I asked him for some suggestions."

"I really like the handle," he said.

"Me, too." She pointed to the blue inlay. "This is lapis. Like the color of your eyes." She knew it was a lovesick thing to say, but she couldn't help it.

"If my eyes are lapis, then yours are malachite." He caught her gaze, then looked down at the knife, tracing the green stones, running his thumb along the intricate pattern they created.

A strong touch. A masculine appreciation.

When he gave her another husbandly kiss, her knees nearly buckled.

Was she imagining his spouselike affection? Building it up in her mind? Or was he as seriously smitten as she was?

Suddenly the oven timer went off.

They separated, and she forced herself to act normal, to return to the kitchen to finish dinner.

She removed the potatoes from the oven and prepared to broil the fillets.

"How do you want your steak?" she called out.

"Medium rare," he called back.

"Is oil and vinegar okay for the salad?"

"Sure. That's fine."

Within no time they sat across from each other, the white candle burning between them. He scanned the table.

"What are you looking for?" she asked.

"Blue cheese dressing."

"You said oil and vinegar was—"

"The blue cheese is for my potato."

She gave him a curious look. "You don't use butter, sour cream or chives?"

"Nope. Just blue cheese dressing. I know there's some in the fridge. I always keep a bottle handy."

"I'll get it for you."

"That's okay. You don't have to wait on me." He got up and went into the kitchen.

When he returned, she watched him dump the dressing onto his potato. He followed the application with a sprinkle of pepper.

"There's still so much I don't know about you," she said.

He glanced up. "Why do you keep saying that?"

"Because it's true."

He squinted at her. "Was I supposed to tell you ahead of time that I put blue cheese on baked potatoes? Is that a major issue?"

"No, of course not." She knew her mind was working overtime. That she probably wasn't making any sense to him. She reached for her water and took a swig. Ethan was watching her, waiting for her to continue.

"Cathy was here today," she said, finding a roundabout way to lead up to her point. "And she confided in me about her parents." Susan scooted forward in her chair. "Why don't you ever talk about your family, Ethan?"

"What's to talk about? You knew my dad way back when. And my mom has been gone since I was a kid."

"That's exactly my point. You've never mentioned her. The things you remember about her. How old you were when she died. That's an important part of who you are."

He just stared at her, still, quiet. Then he frowned. "My mother didn't die."

"I always assumed...I..." She stalled, meeting his troubled gaze. "What happened? Where is she?"

"She split when I was in third grade. She divorced my dad and moved back to New York City, where she was from."

"And you haven't seen her since?"

"No."

"Will you tell me about her?"

"There's no need. It's over. Ancient history."

The pain that crossed his face was like an open

wound, she thought. It wasn't over. "Please, tell me about her."

"Why? What for?"

"Because I want to know." She put down her fork, unable to finish her meal. He'd stopped eating, too. The only things that moved were the flames on the candles. Dancing fire. Dangerous heat.

He didn't give in. "This conversation is a waste of time."

"No, it isn't." She knew she had to admit how she felt, to say the words out loud. "I love you, Ethan. And everything about you is important to me."

A state of panic jumped into his eyes, and he pushed away from the table. "You weren't supposed to do that. You weren't supposed to change the rules."

She held on to her pride, even if her heart was slipping away from her. "Sometimes it seems like you love me, too."

The panic remained in his eyes. "What difference does it make? You'll be leaving soon. Going back to California, back to your old life."

She came to her feet. The candles kept burning, melting, reacting to the flames. "I can stay in Texas. I can relocate. I've already been thinking about it."

"Because of me?"

"Yes."

His voice turned rough. "That's crazy. That's insane. It would never work. You have a job in San Francisco. A career."

"I can run a national hotline from anywhere. I can sell my condo. I can conduct a long-distance relationship with my assistant."

He shook his head. "You'd miss the city. You'd get tired of me. Of being trapped in a small town."

She dropped onto the couch. "That isn't fair. You're comparing me to your mother. To what she did to you."

"Don't analyze me, Susan. Don't do that."

When he rolled his shoulders, she watched the muscles bunch in his arms. Even his veins became too prominent. He was uncomfortable. Wary. And she didn't have the slightest idea how to earn his trust.

"I'm sorry," she said. "I'm sorry if I pushed too hard."

He sat beside her. "I don't want to lose you. But I've known all along that it was going to happen. That we weren't meant to stay together." He reached out to smooth a strand of her hair, but he dropped his hand before he made contact, before he touched her. "This was only supposed to be an affair."

She wanted to cry, to curl up like an embryo.

"I'm throwing myself at you again. Like I did when we were young."

"No, you're not."

"Yes, I am. And you're behaving the same way, too. You're being kind, but you're dodging my advances. Nothing has changed between us. It's the past all over again."

And his rejection pierced her like an arrow, ripping through her skin, stabbing her heart.

"I can't stay here tonight," she told him. "I'm going back to Ryan and Lily's house. I need to be with my family. To stop chasing you."

He fell silent. Sad. Solemn. She waited for him to admit that he loved her. That he couldn't live without her. But he didn't.

In the end, he simply let her go.

Susan spent the next two days milling around Ryan and Lily's house. She told herself she would get over the depression, but at the moment her claim wasn't working.

She sat on the sofa, staring at the TV, where an afternoon talk show went in one ear and out the other. When Lily walked in, she glanced up and tried to smile.

"Is that helping?" Lily asked.

"This?" Susan adjusted the pint of ice cream she was eating. "Vanilla fudge ripple always helps."

Lily took an overstuffed chair. She was getting stronger with each passing day, determined to get past the horror Jason had put her through. "Life's too short to be sad, Susan."

"I know." She used the remote, putting the TV on mute. "I just need to mourn for a while."

"Have you heard from Ethan?"

"No." And she hadn't seen him, either. Not even from afar. She hadn't gone anywhere on the ranch where he might be. "Is Ryan disappointed in us?"

"In you and Ethan?" Lily shook her head. "He thinks you'll get back together."

A lump formed in Susan's throat. Her cousin hadn't gotten over his dream. He was holding on to his beliefs, trying to make his hopes and wishes seem real. "Is he resting?"

"Yes." Lily tucked her legs under her, getting comfortable in the big padded chair. "He had some episodes of confusion today. It's difficult to see him that way, but I've learned to treasure every moment we have left. Even the difficult ones."

"I don't want to leave Ryan," Susan said. "And I don't want to leave you, either. I'll miss both of you so much when I'm gone."

"Then stay. Move into the guesthouse. Live here on the Double Crown."

"I wish I could. But I don't want to put myself in the position of pining after Ethan." In an absent-minded gesture, she stirred the melting ice cream. "It will be easier if I go back to San Francisco."

"Whatever you decide is your choice. But you're always welcome here. Just remember that, okay?"

"Thank you." To keep herself from crying, she lifted the spoon to her mouth, eating another round of calories.

The phone rang. Lily rose to answer it, picking up the portable receiver from an antique desk.

A second later, she mouthed Ethan's name, letting Susan know that he was on the other end of the line.

Her pulse jackknifed. She watched Lily with anticipation, listening to the one-sided conversation.

"I'm doing much better," Lily said. "How are you?" Silence, then, "Let me check." The older woman pressed the hold button, leaving Ethan waiting. "He asked for you," she told Susan. "Do you want to talk to him?"

She considered saying no, but she refused to fall into the jilted-lover trap, playing games that would only end up hurting them both.

Inhaling a gust of air, she set down the ice-cream carton. "Yes, I'll talk to him."

Lily brought her the phone, then left the room, giving her the privacy she needed.

Susan deactivated the hold device. "It's me," she said.

Ethan's voice was quiet. "I just wanted to let you know what was going on." He paused, creating a beat of silence. "Escrow closed early. I got the keys to my new house today."

She loosened her grip on the phone. She'd been squeezing the receiver. "You must be happy about that."

"I am." Another pause. Then he said, "I'd really like you to see it."

She wanted to spare herself the pain of being close to him, but she couldn't say no. She just couldn't. "When?"

"Anytime you're ready. I just left the escrow office, and I'm on my way to the house now."

She pictured him in his truck, driving through town, heading into the country, his cell phone pressed to his ear. "I'll meet you there," she told him, praying she was doing the right thing. "But I need directions."

"Do you have a pen and paper?"

"Not yet." She walked over to the desk and searched for writing utensils, fumbling a little when she found them. "I do now."

She jotted down what he was saying: street names, stops, turns, bends in the road. She doubted that she would get lost. He was being extremely precise.

She repeated the directions, her pulse flitting at her neck. A girlish reaction. Anxiety about seeing him again. "I'll be there as soon as I can."

"Thank you, Susan."

She ended the call, then returned to where she'd left the ice cream. She capped the carton, holding the chilled container against her chest. She could only assume that Ethan needed closure.

A proper way to say goodbye.

To let her go for good.

Ethan resisted the urge to pace, to stalk back and forth like a jungle cat behind bars. So he simply stood in the middle of the vacant house and let his insecurities destroy him.

He glanced out the window and saw that Susan had arrived. He had no idea what he'd been trying to accomplish by inviting her to his new place. All he knew was that he loved her.

And he was scared to death.

She parked behind his truck, and he fought to steady his nerves, to quit being a Freudian basket case.

Anxious, he met her at the front door. For a moment they gazed at each other, the way they'd done so many other times before.

She broke eye contact first, leaving him in an emotional lurch. He wasn't good at fixing his mistakes.

He invited her inside, and she walked into the entryway, her boots sounding on the hardwood floor.

"This is really nice," she said.

"It has more space than I'll need." A home, he thought, that should belong to a family—a father, a mother, a brood of happy, healthy kids.

"Will you give me the grand tour?"

"Sure." He knew this was awkward, uncomfortable for both of them. She looked like a city girl who'd lost her way, and he felt like a cowboy who'd just gotten thrown from his horse. "This is the living room, of course."

"Beamed ceilings and a custom fireplace. You've got good taste, Ethan."

"Thanks." They continued walking, then stopped in the dining room.

She glanced up at the chandelier, and he noticed how pretty she looked. Her blouse was soft and feminine, reminding him of the nightgown she'd worn the first time they'd slept in each other's arms.

They entered the kitchen, where Mexican tiles and oak cabinets prevailed. She commented on the shelf in the windowsill, a sunlit spot to grow herbs and flowers.

A moment later she turned around and caught him watching her. He didn't know what to say, how to explain how mixed-up he was. Just telling her that he loved her wouldn't be enough. He would have to go deeper. He would have to cut a vein and bleed.

"Do you want to see the rest of the house now?" he asked.

She nodded, and they backtracked, crossing rooms they'd already been through to get to the hall. He pointed out the den, the guest bathroom and the extra bedrooms. When they entered the master bedroom, he envisioned her living with him, sharing his life, bearing his children.

She walked over to a sliding-glass door. "You have a beautiful yard." She examined a brick path that led to a redwood gazebo.

He moved closer to her. "Do you want to go outside? There's a little bench out there. We could sit for a while."

"That sounds nice."

A few minutes later they occupied the gazebo. In the distance were the horse amenities, the barn and pastures.

"So this is a gentleman's ranch," she said.

"Yes." But at the moment, he didn't feel like a gentleman. He wished he'd thought to bring some take-out coffee, the flavored kind, with mocha and whipped cream—something sweet and frothy, something to take the edge off an overcast day.

She shifted on the bench. "Your dogs are going to love this place."

"I'm sure they are." Ethan turned to look at her. "Chocolate is going to miss you."

Her breath hitched. "I'm going to miss him, too. And you," she added quietly.

"So will I. You, I mean." He refrained from touching her, from making them both ache. "I miss you already."

"You confuse me, Ethan."

"I confuse myself." He frowned at the acreage that gave him no peace, the land that failed to soothe his soul.

She didn't press him for more information, so he knew he would have to continue on his own. "Do you still want to know about my mom?"

"If you're willing to talk about her."

He kept frowning, the furrow between his eyebrows a burden he couldn't seem to erase. "This will be the first time I've told anyone about her. But I need to do this." He needed to explain why he'd pulled away from Susan. "You were right when you said that I was comparing you to her. I was, but not deliberately. It's just what's inside me. The fear that we'll end up like my parents."

"We're not them. We're us. We're you and me."

"I know. But she screwed with my head when she left. I pretended that she didn't. That she'd hurt my dad worse than she'd hurt me, but I think our pain was equal."

"Did he ever stop loving her?"

"No. And all those years I saw what it did to him."

"How did they meet?" she asked. "How did a girl from New York marry a ranch hand from Texas?"

Ethan glanced at the Valentine heart around Susan's neck. The diamonds glittered like magic. Like fairy dust, he thought. A gift he'd been compelled to buy her.

"My mom was a photography student," he finally said, answering her question. "She was attending a private school. She was raised with money. Not millions, but enough to make her spoiled." He paused to take a breath. "She was working on some sort of thesis project, something to do with the American West. I think she was fascinated with that culture because of her Native ancestry. She went through stages, and that was her cowboys-and-Indians period. So she traveled to Texas for research."

"And became enthralled with your dad?"

"Exactly." Ethan still hadn't quit frowning. "They had this whirlwind affair, and when she returned to New York, they kept in touch, writing letters, making midnight phone calls."

"I can see how she fell for him. Your father was a handsome man."

"And she was a beautiful woman. On the outside, anyway." He glanced at Susan's necklace again. "After she graduated, she got restless, eager for my dad, so she came back to Texas. Her parents were furious, but I think that was part of the thrill. She was rebellious by nature. A live-for-the-moment artist."

"So different from your dad."

"And me. After I was born, her cowboys-and-Indians stage lost its appeal. She couldn't handle being a ranch hand's wife, a stay-at-home mom. She missed New York. She missed not having a career. So she started picking fault with my dad, with me, and the older I got, the more aware I became of it."

Susan met his gaze. "I'm sorry, Ethan."

"Me, too." Sorry he'd let his mom mess with his head. "Dad tried to get her to take pictures of me, to create her art that way, but she wasn't interested in snapping black-and-whites of her kid. I didn't inspire her."

She put her hand on his knee, a gentle touch, a soft comfort. "Your mom didn't deserve you. Or your dad."

"I closed myself off from her, and when she left, I watched my old man fall apart." He covered her hand with his. "And now I'm falling apart."

"You have that right. We all do. Human beings aren't invincible." She locked her fingers through his. "But we're resilient. We bounce back. We heal. We get stronger from the pain."

His eyes burned, but he wasn't about to embarrass himself, to let them water. "I never wanted to be your patient, Susan. To be some whacked-out guy you had to fix."

"You're not my patient. You're the boy who always mattered. The man I fell in love with."

His heartbeat jumped, skittered and skipped. This was his opportunity to start healing, to let the pain go, to trust Susan. "I love you, too," he said, his voice not quite steady. "I'm not sure when it happened. Maybe it was when we were teenagers. Or maybe it happened that night in the rain. I've never been that close to anyone before. Making love, making memories." He snared her gaze, capturing her, holding her captive. "Did you mean what you said? About staying in Texas?"

"Yes." Her eyes misted, and she blinked, a bit furiously, fluttering her lashes, trying to will away the tears.

"Then will you stay? Will you be with me?"

She nodded, and her tears fell. Happy tears, emotional tears.

"I'm so sorry I hurt you." Unable to resist, he caressed her cheek, his fingers grazing her skin. "I shouldn't have let my mom come between us. But I kept seeing myself in my dad."

"Maybe we can visit his grave," she said. "Talk to him, tell him that we found each other."

"I'd like that. And I'm sure he would, too." He

took Susan in his arms, and she fell into his embrace, hugging him, holding him.

Creating another memory.

Another moment he would never forget.

Epilogue

Susan loved the atmosphere. The feminine voices, the girlish chatter, the scent of perfume mingling with the allure of jewels, gems and glitter.

The matron of honor, the bridesmaids and the flower girl were getting ready in the master bedroom in Susan's new home.

And so was she.

She gazed in a full-length mirror, anticipating her walk down the aisle. She'd decided to adhere to tradition, not allowing the groom to see her before the ceremony.

Ethan had proposed to her on February eighteenth, and within ten days they'd planned their wedding, working out every detail. They didn't want to wait; they'd waited long enough to be together. But more than that, they'd forgone a long engagement because they wanted Ryan to have the opportunity to attend their wedding, to give Susan away.

She studied her dress, an elegant white gown with a beaded bodice, delicate embroidery and sweep train.

Lily walked up behind her, and both of their images were reflected in the mirror. "You look beautiful," she said. "A radiant bride."

"Thank you. You look beautiful, too." As the matron of honor, Lily wore a sophisticated ensemble with scattered sequins. The wedding colors suited her well.

Susan had chosen desert blue and Victorian lilac. Accents of yellow were included, as well, adding marigolds and sweet clover to floral arrangements.

"Do you want me to attach your veil?" Lily asked.

She nodded, wondering if this was how Cinderella felt when she'd finally married her prince.

Lily put the veil in place. The sheer fabric shimmered in the light. "Are you nervous?"

"Yes, but in a good way." Susan turned around to face her, and they smiled at each other.

"The rose came off my dress," Cathy said

from another mirror. "Will someone help me pin it back on?"

Kyra, Susan's sister, went to the girl's rescue, reattaching the satin flower. The fourteen-year-old, along with Kyra, was a bridesmaid, and the teenager was thrilled to be part of the ceremony.

In the past ten days Susan had gotten to know Cathy's parents, and she thought they were warm and caring, a loving couple with family values. As for Cathy, she'd become a regular visitor at the Double Crown foaling paddocks. So far she'd attended two births, welcoming adorable little foals into the world.

"It's time," Kyra said suddenly, creating a flurry of satin and lace.

Susan's pulse jumped to her throat. The wedding procession was about to begin. She glanced at her sister, and they exchanged a sibling smile. Kyra looked breathtaking, but she always did.

The bridesmaids exited the sliding-glass door, heading for the gazebo. Susan and Ethan had chosen that as their wedding site. Although the bench had been removed, flowers and plants and a makeshift altar had been added.

Lily fanned Susan's veil one last time, then followed the bridesmaids. Susan noticed that her cousin was already getting teary eyed.

The flower girl went next, carrying a silk basket and taking careful steps in her pretty white shoes.

Finally Susan slipped outside, knowing Ryan was there, eager to do his part. He reached for her arm, and they waited for the organist to play her song.

"My baby girl," he said to her.

She studied his face, the lines near his eyes, the aging texture of his skin. She knew this was one of the happiest moments of his life. He'd predicted her wedding all along. "You helped make this dream come true."

"I did, didn't I?" He gave her a matchmaker's wink.

"The Wedding March" began, announcing the bride, and they moved forward, walking down the aisle.

They passed a sea of guests, and a moment later she glanced up and saw Ethan, waiting at the altar, his expression filled with awe.

A symphony of butterflies took flight, swirling in her stomach. He looked tall and handsome in a Western tuxedo, with a full satin yoke and bolo tie. On his lapel he sported a lavender rose.

Ryan offered her to the groom, and she took her place beside him. When he smiled at her, the butterflies disappeared. She returned his smile, then handed her bouquet to Lily, preparing for the rest of the ceremony.

To marry the man she loved.

Soon they exchanged vows. Traditional verses.

A lifelong commitment. Susan meant every word, and she knew Ethan did, too.

The rings came next. His was a wide white-gold band, and hers glittered with diamonds, complementing the Valentine necklace she wore.

When he leaned in to kiss her, he touched her veil, and the fabric fluttered between them.

They separated, and he looked into her eyes. Captivated, she saw their future: erotic nights, early morning coffee, brand-new babies, the dogs and horses that would always be part of their lives.

Together, they turned to face their guests, presenting themselves as Mr. and Mrs. Eldridge.

Best friends, she thought. Thriving lovers.

Husband and wife.

* * * * *

FAMOUS FAMILIES

YES! Please send me the *Famous Families* collection featuring the Fortunes, the Bravos, the McCabes and the Cavanaughs. This collection will begin with 3 FREE BOOKS and 2 FREE GIFTS in my very first shipment— and more valuable free gifts will follow! My books will arrive in 8 monthly shipments until I have the entire 51-book *Famous Families* collection. I will receive 2-3 free books in each shipment and I will pay just $4.49 U.S./$5.39 CDN for each of the other 4 books in each shipment, plus $2.99 for shipping and handling.* If I decide to keep the entire collection, I'll only have paid for 32 books because 19 books are free. I understand that accepting the 3 free books and gifts places me under no obligation to buy anything. I can always return a shipment and cancel at any time. My free books and gifts are mine to keep no matter what I decide.

268 HCN 9971   468 HCN 9971

Name _____ (PLEASE PRINT) _____

Address _____ Apt. # _____

City _____ State/Prov. _____ Zip/Postal Code _____

Signature (if under 18, a parent or guardian must sign)

Mail to the **Reader Service:**
IN U.S.A.: P.O. Box 1867, Buffalo, NY 14240-1867
IN CANADA: P.O. Box 609, Fort Erie, Ontario L2A 5X3